london is
the best city
in america

 This Large Print Book carries the
Seal of Approval of N.A.V.H.

london is
the best city
in america

laura dave

Thorndike Press • Waterville, Maine

Published in 2006 by arrangement with Viking, a division of Penguin Group (USA) Inc.

Thorndike Press® Large Print Core.

The tree indicium is a trademark of Thorndike Press.

The text of this Large Print edition is unabridged. Other aspects of the book may vary from the original edition.

Set in 16 pt. Plantin.

Printed in the United States on permanent paper.

Library of Congress Cataloging-in-Publication Data

Dave, Laura.
    London is the best city in America / by Laura Dave.
        p. cm. — (Thorndike Press large print core)
    ISBN 0-7862-8752-7 (lg. print : hc : alk. paper)
        1. Young women — Fiction. 2. Rhode Island — Fiction.
    3. Large type books. I. Title. II. Serices: Thorndike Press large print core series.
    PS3604.A938L66 2006b
        813′.6—dc22   2006011164

to my parents;
and my brother

acknowledgments

For such stellar guidance, insight, and unending faith in me, I am deeply grateful to my editors Carole DeSanti and Molly Barton; my agent Gail Hochman; and Dana Forman, this book's first friend.

The all-stars: Sylvie Rabineau; Beena Kamlani, Carolyn Coleburn, Nancy Sheppard, and Carolyn Horst at Viking; Marianne Merola and Joanne Brownstein at Brandt and Hochman; and Gwyn Lurie.

The know-it-alls: Gayle Walsch; Rick Blanchard; Bill Dittmar of Bully Boy Bullmastiffs; Camrin Crisci; my wonderful teachers at the University of Virginia and the University of Pennsylvania; and Jeremy Church — my favorite fisherman.

My fantastic, first readers: Elizabeth Weinstein; Julie Farkas; Jessica Bohrer; Nick Breslow; Shannan Rouss; and Ben Tishler.

Supporters of every variety: Ben Cramer; Carolyn Marie Janiak; Meg Blevins; Vicki Brand; Bonnie Carrabba; Andrew Cohen; Brett Forman; Jenny Kennedy; Jenni Lapidus; Dot Lasky; Caitlin Leffel; Lisa Menitoff; Whitney Pellegrino; Melissa Rice; Becca Richards; Jill Schwartzman; Courtenay Seabring; Shauna Seliy; Josh Ufberg; and Maggie Vining.

The people and places that made writing a first novel possible: the Henry Hoyns Fellowship; the Tennessee Williams Scholarship; Jody Donohue Associates; The Ventana Inn in Big Sur; The Writers Room; 71 Irving; and my great editors at *Self Magazine* and *ESPN the Magazine*.

If you are not too long,
I will wait here for you all my life.
— Oscar Wilde

Narragansett, Rhode Island

She told herself that if he touched her one time, she wouldn't leave. She told herself that if in his sleep tonight, he reached for her, or put his hand on her leg, his hand on her knee, his face near her face, his leg against her leg, his mouth against her back, his palm on her stomach, his arm on her hip, his hip beside her leg, his head beneath her shoulders, his cheek along her neck — she would stick it out. All these options, he had! And Emmy would stick it out forever. Stay put, stay faithful, stay here.

Where was here? Not home. They weren't home. It was the Friday before Independence Day and a hundred degrees outside, and they were in a highway motel in southern Rhode Island, on their way to his parents' in Maine for the long weekend. They hadn't planned on stopping, but they had left the city late because her meeting with their wedding planner had run late,

11

and then he had been annoyed. And then she had been annoyed because — did she really need to remind him? — she hadn't wanted a wedding planner in the first place, had wanted just the two of them on a cliff somewhere, maybe New Mexico, high above sea level, adobe houses seeping into dry land.

Emmy turned over onto her back. The sheets were stiff here. The fire alarm was right above her head. The television remote was next to her. The ordering went: her, television remote, him. He was on his back too. She could turn on the television and it wouldn't wake him. She could get up and get dressed and go get a Coke at the vending machine and it wouldn't wake him. She could sit with her Coke by the indoor pool for an hour or two hours and her absence wouldn't wake him.

If he happened to wake up by himself and see that she was gone, he would be worried, but not so worried that he'd come look for her. He would take a shower first. He would listen to the radio and get a traffic update. He would call his family to give them an estimated time of arrival. He would wait.

It used to be another way. Emmy knew this. Just like she knew that if she left today, she would lose him. She was losing him slowly anyway. But if she left today, she would lose him quickly and entirely. Her devotion had been enough to ward that off so far. To keep them together. Matt was loyal to that type of devotion. He was marrying her, wasn't he? He'd keep showing up for her and sleeping with her and spending his time with her, and maybe if she paid less attention to him, she wouldn't see that he wasn't in love with her anymore. Maybe, after time, she could convince herself that he was at least something close to in love with her, or he could convince himself of the same thing. And she could go on, the way she had been going on — both having him and longing for him.

But not if she left today. If she left today, he would need to go to his parents' alone and tell them what had happened. He'd need to stand there by himself and explain that she had disappeared on him. He'd need to give them reasons why. For all of these things, he would never forgive her.

At six a.m., Matt turned onto his side, his back toward her. His hands were somewhere beneath the sheets. Emmy crawled out of bed and went into the bathroom. She brushed her teeth and washed her face and pulled her hair into a bun. She had long brown hair that she washed in horse shampoo to keep it soft. She put on the peach sundress she had been wearing the day before. She had very pale skin, which didn't look so good beneath peach. It looked better beneath blues and ivories and reds.

Her suitcase was already packed, so she took it. She left him the car keys and the car. She closed the door behind herself. She stopped at the front desk to pay for the room. She wanted to leave him a note, but she didn't know what to say. So she got another room key from the day manager and let herself back into the room and took off her peach dress and got back into bed with him.

Now they were face to face.

A little before nine, his eyes fluttered open. Still, green eyes. He looked at her.

She reached out and touched his cheek, first with the outsides of her fingers, then with the insides.

"Did you know it's supposed to rain later?" she asked.

Matt shook his head no. He yawned.

"It is," she said. "Big-time. Big storm. It should cool things down a bit."

He nodded, his eyes starting to close

again. This, of course, was only his preliminary wake-up. There would be another two, maybe three, until one took. She wouldn't be around for those. She took off her engagement ring and put it on the pillow and got back out of bed and put back on her peach sundress and picked up her suitcase again and walked out the hotel room door again, and this time she did it forever.

part one

Three Years Later

The main jetty in Point Judith, Rhode Island, is long and narrow. Early enough on any weekday morning it isn't uncommon to see a few people lined up along it, waving a final good-bye to the fishermen who are pulling out of port to sea. It is for luck that they do this: they stand there until the fishermen make their way past the last marker — past that last mark — drifting completely out of sight. That is, except, on the first Friday morning of any month, when Jesse O'Brien's lobster boat pulls out of that port. Then his girlfriend, Betsy, stands there waving for only for a minute before running away herself. This way, Jesse is the one who ends up having to watch her leave him.

From the back room of the small bait and tackle shop, I'd watched Betsy make her full-speed run off that jetty several times. It was one of the few perks of working there: the view of the jetty, and the larger-than-life fishing boats — the pale blue ocean lumbering out farther than I knew how to see. It was a perfect view. And it almost made up for what I could see from the shop's front room — the dusty roadside with its power lines and windblown debris, and the small highway motel that I had walked out of exactly three years before.

The truth is that after my dramatic exit from the motel room, I didn't slink far. Just down the highway, two lefts — first onto South Pier Road, then Ocean Road — right into the main part of town, the pier, where I found a different motel room (which I paid for, immediately, through the next week) and took a shower, and lay down on my back, on the floor, trying to figure out what to do next.

I had no idea what to do next. Eventually, though, I got off the floor and headed back outside, and took a very long walk along the ocean, and decided that if someone were going to pick a place to be self-stranded, this beach town wasn't a bad one to choose.

Things seemed to just happen from there. Within the first few days, I found a house-sitting gig in a guesthouse up on

Boston Neck Road, the main road that ran straight into town, along the pier, all the way up to the university. It wasn't quite an oceanside house, but close to being an oceanside house. And in exchange for light housework, I had free rein with the mostly unfurnished 3,000-square-foot guesthouse: a place I rarely left with the exception of weekday mornings, when I'd drive down to the other end of Narragansett, where I became the assistant manager (aka only employee) at the tackle shop. This was *not* the famous tackle shop — the one connected to the equally famous seafood restaurant, and frequented by tourists and party fishers and summer people who owned boats with names like *So F-In Happy.* It was the other one, the one on the far end of the docks, the raggedy one nestled in right by the water tower.

Today, I was hanging there long after my shift ended — just circling the back room — long after Betsy came and disappeared. It seemed better than the alternative, which I was forced to remember every time my eyes fixed on my boss's Porsche-of-the-month calendar hanging on the wall. I had circled today's date in bright red marker. July 4. Independence Day. In the "4" square, I had written —

21

ny. In small, small letters.

"Hey, Manhattan." I turned toward the back room's doorway, leading storefront, to see Bobby, the shop's owner, with two steel fishing rods in one hand, a bucket of Dum Dum lollipops in the other.

Bobby was sixty-seven, recently remarried to the same wife for the third time, and regularly annoyed at everyone in the world except for me, even if he did still refer to me by the nickname — Manhattan — that he had coined my first day on the job. He was always especially angry at the shop's few loyal customers, whom he blamed for keeping him from the retirement he'd been talking about since before his wife came back to him for round two. Weekly, he'd remind me to look for a new job. Daily, he'd say that we'd soon be closing down for good.

"Aren't you supposed to be on your way home by now?" How could I answer? I was. I really was.

"I'm just bracing myself," I said.

He gave me a look, which I ignored. What I was bracing myself for was this: my brother Josh was getting married. I needed to start driving toward suburban New York, toward my childhood home, for his wedding. But I just couldn't bear the endless questions that I knew would come my way as soon as I walked into wedding-weekend territory: What's your personal life like? When are *you* getting married? What's your plan after leaving Rhode Island? And what, again, are you still doing there?

"Would you mind bracing yourself out front then?" he asked. "We've got overflow."

Overflow, for us, was more than two customers. A quick peek out front revealed we had three. This included a young waitress from the fancy seafood restaurant/tackle shop, who liked to come over to us during her breaks. I wasn't quite sure why. In three years, I'd never seen her buy anything. Not even a Dum Dum.

Who was I to judge? From the beginning, no one back home understood all the time I was spending in this tackle shop — or my decision to stay in Rhode Island at all, for that matter. So I came up with a legitimate reason for sticking around. I decided to make a documentary about the wives of offshore fishermen. Where better to do that than in a fishing town? I thought it would be interesting to take a look at all these women who were constantly being left. Who were needing to take care of everything alone again for one, two, three months at a time while their husbands were off at sea. Who were, ultimately, in a constant state of waiting.

It seemed liked a very good idea, at first. But all these years later, the project wasn't exactly where I'd hoped it would be. Where anyone could rightfully expect it to be. This was in no small part due to the fact that while I had initially planned on interviewing just a couple of wives to keep the project manageable — four or five wives, tops — I had moved *a little* beyond my initial subject pool.

I was on wife 107.

At last count.

Somewhere along the line, it had all just gotten so warped in my head. The different wives all starting to blend into each other — blond hair becoming brown, cigarettes becoming bitten-down fingernails, tattoos becoming reading glasses — until I couldn't see them at all anymore. Three Amys and four Jens and six Christinas and one Daisy and seven Jills and two Laurens and four Lindas and three Gayles and five Josies and three Ninas and four Theresas and one Carrie and five Nicoles and six Emilys and eight Maggies and four Dianes and three Kristies and two Sues and four

Beths and nine Julies and three Maras and seven Lucys and two Junes and five Kates and two Lornas and four Saras — and I couldn't see anything they were telling me. Not any of them.

All I could see, still, was Matt.

Bobby readjusted the lollipop bucket in his arms. "You know what, Manhattan? Forget it. Just get going already. Weddings wait for no man. Believe me." He turned to head back out to the front.

The clock on the wall said 3:35 p.m. I was supposed to meet my brother at the Scarsdale Pool in exactly four hours and ten minutes to watch the fireworks. I had promised Josh, promised my whole family, that I'd be home in time for that. Considering the inevitable holiday weekend traffic I was about to face, if I didn't leave right now, my lateness would be the first thing I'd need to explain.

From the shop's back exit to the driver's side of my car takes forty-eight seconds. I knew this now because I counted as I went — nine fast paces across the parking lot, closing the car door behind me, adjusting the rearview mirror, buckling myself in. It stopped me from thinking for a minute. But then I saw all my bags in the backseat of my car, the greater half of everything I owned staring back at me, and I still couldn't help but wonder if I'd forgotten something important. If I'd forgotten the one thing that would tell everyone I was okay. What *was* the one thing that I thought would convince them I was doing just fine, here, on my own? A short-sleeved purple sweater? That seemed doubtful.

I put my car in reverse, pulling out of the parking lot just as June Martin (aka June #2) was making a left into it, riding close to the wheel in her red Volvo station wagon. Her kids weren't in the backseat, but all of their things were clogging up the back windows, the trunk windows even: car seats and balloons, candy-food wrappers, stuffed toys.

June had three girls: Dana, Carolyn, and Holly. Tomorrow was the youngest one's birthday party. June brought an invitation to me at the shop last week. It was still in my glove compartment — all pink and shiny — like a leftover wish. When you were hoping to attend a kid's birthday party, you knew you were in trouble.

"You going this way?" June mouthed, pointing in the direction of my house, moving her wagon forward so I could make the right that way.

But I pointed in the other direction, pointed — with something like reluctance or resolve — in the direction of the highway, and New York.

"This way," I mouthed back, giving her a small smile, a wave good-bye. She waved back. Then I headed where I said I would.

I was going home.

Here's the thing about going home again.

You don't always know what you'll remember. And, still, it was starting to seem to me that — if you paid close enough attention — you could sometimes predict moments that were going to turn out to be important, moments that would stay with you. There had been at least a dozen times over the course of my childhood that I had gone with my brother Josh to the Scarsdale Pool to watch the fireworks on July 4. If you wanted to watch Independence Day fireworks in my hometown, there weren't a whole lot of other options. But tonight, from the moment we arrived, it felt different. We were sitting in our usual spot on the hillside — looking down over the main pool, a little outside of the main crowd — when everything started moving into this bizarrely sharp, almost etched focus. And suddenly I felt oddly aware of how clear the sky was, how blond and happy the family on the blanket next to us was, how everything was bright and fluid even while it was happening — already existing closer to memory than reality. It was like a warning shot that something intense was coming.

And even though I had agreed to go to the fireworks — had agreed to sit on that small hill and eat hot dogs and watch the bright colors in the sky — part of me wanted to suggest we leave right then, get out early and beat the crowds to the parking lot, head home. Because given the right set of circumstances, given an intense moment, those things can certainly mess with you — fireworks and clear air and happiness — can make you think the world is a way it isn't, can make you say things that, on another night, you would never say.

That Josh would never say. Such as: "I'm not sure I'm doing the right thing. You know, getting married this weekend."

I turned and looked at him in disbelief. He was staring straight ahead, taking a bite of his hot dog. It was enough to make me think I'd imagined what I'd heard. That I'd made it up. I mean — who would eat a bite of hot dog right after saying something like that? A crazy person. My brother wasn't crazy. At least I hadn't thought so.

But then it happened again.

"Emmy," he started — using my name this time, emphasizing the "m" sound the way he'd always do, turning my name into one small letter. "Are you going to just pretend you didn't hear me?"

"You were chewing," I said.

"Not until after. Don't ignore me."

One of the first things Josh ever taught me, maybe the very first, was that you absolutely had to ignore everything you weren't ready to deal with. It was your only shot of keeping it at bay. Like the first day of school, for instance. This was his favorite example. If no one talked about the first day, he'd say — if no one planned it or agreed to it or worked toward it — it couldn't happen. How could it happen? What a little genius he'd been! If everyone had just shut up about school starting, it could have stayed summer forever.

I put my hot dog down, wiping my hands on my jeans. "I'm not ignoring you, Josh," I said. "I'm listening."

"Because there might be a problem here," he said. "I love Meryl and everything, but there really might be a big problem."

In demonstration, he made a "big" rectangle sign with his hands, his hot dog in one of them, a large Coke cup in the other. The little girl from the blond family was staring at him. I wondered what she thought she saw — this child-man in his dirty baseball cap, white button-down shirt, bare feet. My big brother. Best friend since birth. Childhood hero. Huge baby. He was going to be thirty-one next month. In less than seventy-two hours, he was supposed to be someone's husband. Someone who, even if it wasn't the point, I really loved.

"Does this problem have a name, Josh?" I asked.

He was quiet for a long minute in which I got to imagine that my instinct was wrong. Maybe this had nothing to do with another woman. It would be easier if it didn't. I figured that he'd be more likely to get married this weekend if it didn't have something to do with that.

"Elizabeth," he said.

My heart dropped. I could actually feel it — the hollowing out of it — until it filled my whole stomach, like a drum. I couldn't remember having heard about anyone named Elizabeth from him, not during the year he'd spent alone in Boston, not since I'd been living in Rhode Island. The fact

31

that he'd kept her to himself made her seem bigger, somehow, more important.

"Elizabeth?" I said.

"Elizabeth, yes. Elizabeth."

I couldn't look at him, not when he wasn't looking back at me. I stared at the main pool instead, blocked off with a fat orange rope so that nobody could fall in. Or jump. One of the first times Josh brought Meryl home with him, we swam in this pool — all three of us, together. She was wearing this backless green bathing suit that revealed a thin line of freckles right along her spine. I was only sixteen. I'd never seen anything like that.

"She has no idea, does she?" I said.

"Meryl?" He shook his head. "No, I don't think so."

"You sure?"

"Pretty sure."

I didn't know what to say then. It all felt too crazy. I was supposed to be Meryl's maid of honor on Sunday. I had a long blue sheath dress with thin straps. I had a pearl necklace I never would wear otherwise. I had white lily hairpins. Josh had encouraged all of this.

"You want pizza?" Josh said. "I want to get a slice of pizza before we leave. And another soda."

"You think the snack bar's even open still?"

"I think it could be."

Then he stood up. I shielded my eyes against the night sky, staring up at him. I had a million questions to ask, but none that I was particularly ready to hear the answers to.

"What, Emmy?" he said, looking down at me.

"I just want to know how you can be so sure," I said. "That Meryl doesn't know? I mean, how can you know that?"

"Didn't we just cover this?" he said.

There was an edge to his voice. He wasn't good at disappointing people, which I could already guess was at least part of the reason that he was in the position he was in now. He couldn't seem to tell anyone no, even when that was exactly what was needed.

"I'm just trying to understand," I said, as he sat back down.

"Which part?"

"How you got here," I said.

He didn't say anything, but lay all the way back on the grass, covering his eyes with his arm.

I swatted at him. "Come on. Go get your pizza before the thing closes."

He shook his head. "I don't want it anymore."

"You don't want it anymore?"

"No," he said.

"What do you want, Josh?"

"Something else," he said.

Who once said that, in any family, there was one child who was better at things, even if exactly how much better was never spoken? There was the one who got the better grades and did better at sports, who things just came easier for. It seemed to me that, usually, it was the older one who would tread the straighter path, whose initial accomplishments would run deeper. Could it be just a coincidence that so many of the great sufferers — those who would eventually take to art and writing and music and dance — were younger or youngest siblings? Joyce and Twain and Austen and Baryshnikov. Were they always feeling like they were just in a game of catch-up they had already lost?

I never had any illusion of ever being able to catch up. In our family, at least, Josh was always quicker than I was. He was the one that made all the all-star teams and got straight A's, the one who knew who he wanted to be. His goals might have changed a little over the years, but only in the most assured and boring way: pediatrician, brain surgeon, pediatrician again. He never had any inappropriate ideas like joining the circus or moving to Alaska. At fifteen, Josh was already taking a psychology class at the community college, looking into seven-year medical programs, telling our parents' dinner guests coyly about his plans. And he was certainly always the one who was better at relationships. He had been with Meryl for the better part of the decade, and it appeared to be fairly smooth sailing for the two of them: maintenance during the end of college, all through Josh's medical school and residency, well into their current cohabitation in Los Angeles.

My own relationship history was a little messier, more dramatic, which — whether or not it's the nicest thing to say about myself — was also a fairly accurate way to describe the behavior that landed me in the second-place position. While Josh was navigating the straight and possible, I spent most of my younger years conjuring up situations for myself that could never be: becoming a dancer in Brazil (I was relegated to the back row in after-school ballet class), marrying a rock star (cigarette smoke at concerts made my eyes swell closed), running a cruise ship (tendency to get seasick in port).

But Josh and Meryl — they had always made sense. Even how they met was such a nice story, so in want of a happy ending. It was the night of Halloween during their senior year of college. Meryl was having a party at her house off-campus, and Josh went dressed as a frog (my idea: kiss the frog and he'll turn into a prince). He had gone to the party because he liked one of Meryl's roommates. Would you believe me if I told you she was dressed like a princess? Meryl, not the roommate. From the very beginning then, Josh would later say, he wasn't sure he deserved her. But Meryl's boyfriend — who was away at medical school — didn't make it back for the party even though he had promised to. So she found herself sad in the bathroom, having broken up with him earlier that day or the day before. They'd argue over the actual moment — *don't you think I'd know, he was my boyfriend?* — as if that was the interesting part. The interesting part, if you ask me, was that they spent the whole night in the bathroom, frog and sad princess, while someone in desperation was throwing up outside, trying to open the door. That part's not interesting, Josh liked to say. That's disgusting.

Here's the only part of them, of my brother and Meryl, that I found myself questioning during those years after they graduated from school: Why were they waiting so long — through year after year of close friends tying the knot — to get married themselves? They lived together out in Los Angeles, already existing in a fairly married state. But Josh said that neither of them was really in a rush to "make it official." His words, not mine. One of the main reasons he offered for this non-rush was that Meryl took wedding pictures for a living, which seemed to considerably lower her threshold for thinking in any detail about her own big day.

This seemed like a plausible explanation, especially because, even once Meryl started planning her wedding, she made it very clear that she wanted to keep the wedding low-key: family, a few friends, a small tent in my parents' backyard. In my parents' backyard. She was most adamant about this part. Maybe this was partially due to the fact that her own family situation was a little complicated. Her parents — Bess and Michael, the parents who raised her — lived on the Upper East Side of Manhattan in a duplex that wrapped around two city blocks. Her birth parents, on the other hand, were sociology professors at a small college in the Ozark Mountains. As far as anyone could tell — until Meryl had found them a few years before — they hadn't spent any time to speak of away from the Ozark Mountains. But now they too were en route to this weekend's wedding. An *entire* wedding weekend.

How had that happened? How had Meryl's plans for an intimate family-only wedding turned into a full-blown extended celebration? No one was exactly sure, but it had something to do with her decision to let Bess take over the majority of the planning. Bess turned the reception into a three-hundred-person affair at the Essex House in New York City, complete with a ten-piece band and a cocktail hour and a very expensive pineapple cake.

Then my mother — in an attempt to give Meryl and Josh what they had originally wanted — decided to host a fifty-person rehearsal dinner in our backyard, which was now taking place tomorrow night.

And tonight, post-fireworks, I had

helped organize a small late-night bachelor party at a local bar for Josh. The bachelor party was my apology, in a way, for being so absent over the course of the wedding planning. Josh and Meryl had been so far away out in California — me, just a few hours from New York City by car. I could have stepped in and tried to negotiate things with Bess, tried to shrink the massive party planning. But I hadn't. Not that Josh had complained once about this. Meryl wouldn't let him. She understood that I couldn't really come back to New York, not yet. She understood that even after Josh thought it was time I did. Even after everyone else in my life thought it was time I did too. I felt myself starting to panic and turned to Josh. I needed to talk him through this. I needed to hear him talk.

"Josh," I said. "What are you going to do?"

He didn't answer me. He didn't even move. I tried to think of what I really wanted to say to him. Already, I'd made him feel alone in this. I didn't want to make it worse. But, still, it didn't make much sense to me. This was him. This was Meryl and him. For a decade now. For forever now. That first day the three of us had come to this pool together, I forgot to put on sunblock and severely burned the tops of my feet and toes. Meryl had made a pail for me of vinegar and oatmeal. She told me that it would take the sting out. She sat there until the red went down.

"I mean, I'm on your side. Of course I'm on your side. I just hope you're considering everything that needs to be considered, you know? People get scared to get married. They get really scared. How many movies start with someone running the wrong way down the aisle?"

I looked down at him, waiting for a response. But he didn't say anything. He didn't even move his arm off his eyes. And upon closer inspection, I realized that his chest was moving up and down a little too steadily, his eyes closed tightly beneath his bent arm.

I poked him hard in the ribs.

He shot up, startled. "What?" he said. "What's the matter?"

It made me mad. I was here contemplating his future, and he was sleeping. This was what he did, though — this was how he did things. Sleeping was his main defense mechanism, like running away, for someone else, or pretending not to understand. Or maybe I was giving him too much credit. Maybe he was just that unin-volved.

"You asked me a question," I said. "You asked if I was ready to go home."

"Are you?" he said, confused.

I handed him his flip-flops.

"Very," I said.

It was hard for me to think about Josh and Meryl without also thinking about Matt and me. Beyond the arguably analogous situation Josh had managed to find himself in now, my brother's situation with Meryl had often, in other ways, mirrored my situation with Matt. Or, maybe I should say, our situation matched theirs. For one thing, it was exactly a year to the day after Josh met Meryl that I first met Matt. The reason I remember this for certain is that we, too, met the night of Halloween — the Halloween following their first meeting, actually — a coincidence that I found a little bizarre at the time. But over the years since, I kept meeting people who had a Halloween either at the beginning or the end of their relationship.

And I started to think that maybe it wasn't bizarre at all — maybe it just made a certain kind of sense that it would be

43

easier for people to act most like themselves when they were pretending to be someone else. This could also begin to explain why so many old-school wedding superstitions were wrapped up in All Hallows' Eve. Young brides-to-be used to stand around a fire holding stringed apples over the flames. Legend went that the young woman whose apple fell would marry first and have the longest and happiest union. The one whose apple fell last would have the toughest time. Young grooms, meanwhile, would crawl under a blackberry bush in their costumes. And when they reached the other side, they would receive instructions on whether their union was fated for bliss or destruction. Forever now, apparently, relationships coming together or falling apart based on what ghosts said.

The Halloween that Matt and I met, I was in my last year of high school and already planning way past my hometown. I'd only applied to schools on the other side of the country, imagining sunshine, California convertible tops, people who would think New York sounded both exotic and absolutely unappealing. People that would lead me to my new life.

But there I was — still in my hometown — standing at the Scarsdale train station wearing jeans and a ponytail and a short sweater. I had wandered off from the party down the street to get some liters of soda and was using the pay phone, calling over there for someone to come and bring me back. This was when I saw him. He was in the train station entryway smoking a cigarette, wearing a pair of army pants and a paint-splattered white T-shirt. Blue streaks were covering both cheeks. He kept his eyes down, his long eyelashes steady. He was, without a doubt, my favorite thing I'd ever seen.

I put the phone down. "What are you supposed to be over there?" I asked. "A painter?"

This was my great pickup line.

He looked up at me, caught my eyes, started to smile, his cheek-to-cheek, once-in-a-blue-moon smile. And then he stopped. "What are you supposed to be over there?" he asked back. "A high school prep?"

As it turned out, Matt wasn't dressed up either. His parents had just moved to Scarsdale — his mom had just had another kid, a little boy — and he had come out for the day from the city, from NYU, where he was just starting his sophomore year.

Where he had just declared a major in architecture. A minor in still drawing. He had spent the day helping his dad paint their new basement. The only reason he accepted my invite to come back with me to my friend's party was that he had missed his train back to the city and had an hour to kill until the next one. Later, he'd tell me this, not to be mean, but because he found it amazing how far we'd come. Even by the end of that first night. I didn't care about any of that anyway. All I knew was that he reached for the soda.

"I'm coming with you," he said slowly. "Just show me where it is you want to go."

By the time Josh and I made it out of the front parking lot — past the Welcome to the Municipal Pool sign — it was almost a half hour later. All the happy energy of the fireworks was left somewhere behind: everyone honking at each other and squeezing each other in. One SUV that was holding about seven kids broke down in the parking lot's main intersection, all of them crying hysterically as the people yelled at them to get out of the way.

Josh was driving my car. When he finally took the left out of the parking lot, we were less than ten minutes from my parents' house — Mamaroneck Road opening up all around us: the soccer fields on our right, houses banking up on the left, long silvery driveways locked down behind bushes and gates.

Things looked so different to me, being back there. They *seemed* so different than they'd been in the years since I'd left — everything brighter, shinier. More gates. It definitely seemed closer to the Scarsdale that you hear about on television or in the movies than the Scarsdale that I remembered. When I was growing up here, there seemed to be more money problems, more people dressing down. Maybe that wasn't accurate, or I just wasn't paying attention then in the way I could now that I lived on the other side of it. And still, I didn't like seeing the newly minted cars, fluorescent mailboxes. I didn't remember the professional dog walkers. Like anywhere, I guess, there were so many great things about growing up in my hometown, and some less than great things. I wasn't a great athlete, to put it mildly, and a lot of the childhood wars in Scarsdale seemed to be fought and won on soccer fields and basketball courts. Even though I participated, I couldn't get too revved up about it. I couldn't, for a long time, get too revved up about anything, convinced as I was that my life, in whatever capacity it would one day exist, wouldn't truly start until sometime after Scarsdale was behind me.

Maybe what I could say about my hometown, without much hesitation, was that it was more chock-full of signs than any other place I'd ever seen. Don't walk, Dangerous Curve, Duck Crossing, No Parking Around Corner, Stop Sign Ahead, Yield 100 ft. Every block, every half a block. More instructions on how you are — and aren't — allowed to live.

Josh took a left onto our parents' street, not pulling the wheel tightly enough so that the left blinker stopped its persistent blinking. It was still making its loud clucking noises, happily flashing away.

"Have you noticed," he said, "that this place has gotten flashier in the last few years? All these families, do you think they got together and decided that putting terra-cotta sculptures in their front yards was a good idea?"

"I can't believe you just said terra-cotta," I said.

"Like today in the village," he continued, ignoring me. "As an example. This very loud redheaded woman was screaming at her friend from across the street about what kind of scooped-out bagel she wanted. Cinnamon raisin. Doesn't that scoop out all the raisins?"

"That could be anywhere, Josh," I said.

"But it wasn't," he said. "It was here."

My parents' house was coming up on the right. It looked exactly the same to me as it always had — a two-story white Victorian with green shutters, a balcony, screened-in wraparound porch with large plants. I could see the edge of the backyard, which was rocky and curved upward into a small hill. When I was little, I'd thought it was a mountain.

The blinker was still going. "Hey, you have to flip the wheel harder than that, or it's never going to stop," I said, pointing at the dashboard.

He looked down, pulling the wheel as tight as it would go, the clicking shutting down.

"You shouldn't be driving around like this. You can't have a broken blinker. Let's go over to Billy's and see if he'll take a look at it. Isn't he open until midnight on week-ends?"

I looked at the dashboard clock. It said 10:48. Josh was supposed to be at the Heathcote Tavern a half hour ago. He was supposed to be having drinks with his friends and telling stories and being a little too happy for himself. Now, considering the knowledge I'd recently acquired, I wasn't sure if he should even try to pull that off.

"You can pretend to be sick tonight, you know," I said.

"Why would I do that?"

"No reason," I said, though I could think of twelve right off the top of my head, high on the list being that he didn't seem particularly certain that a wedding was even going to take place.

"Don't go stirring the pot, Emmy. I love Meryl. You know I do. I don't want to do anything to ruin this weekend for her."

"I know, but, Josh, if you're thinking about not getting married . . ."

He turned the ignition off. "Who said anything about not getting married? I never said that. Who do you think I am, you?"

I let that go.

"And don't go saying anything to Mom either," he said. "She has enough to worry about with the rehearsal dinner tomorrow night. She has enough going on. You know what I'm saying?"

I actually had no idea what he was saying. And I really didn't know how we were getting lost in wedding logistics again, on the tail end of what he had told me under an hour ago.

Only there didn't seem to be much for me to do about it now. Josh was already out of the car, and heading up to the house. I closed my own door quickly, hurrying to catch up to him anyway.

"I shouldn't have said anything in the first place," he said, as I fell into step with him. "Just please don't say her name again."

"Which one?" I said.

He gave me a dirty look, and I looked down at the ground, at our feet, mine so small next to his, barely half their size. Josh had always been the one who had taken care of me, *always*, even when he hadn't wanted to: the one who had to walk me to the bus stop everyday, the first one to babysit me, the one to teach me how to play kickball, how to lie to our parents (poorly, but still), how to drive. I couldn't shake the feeling that, for the first time, maybe, he was the one who needed the taking care of. And that, somehow, he needed me to do it.

"I just don't believe you would tell me what you told me if you wanted to pretend it didn't matter," I said.

51

He stopped walking, reaching for my arm. "Why are you pushing this? Don't you want me to marry Meryl? Wouldn't that be the happy ending here?"

"It doesn't matter what I want, Josh," I said.

He didn't say anything.

"I'm just trying to understand what's going on with you."

"Well, I'll tell you what," he said. "I'll go ahead and put that on my list of things to figure out, okay?"

Then he gave me a small, sad smile and started walking again toward the dim light of our front porch.

It seems important to mention that this was only the third time I had been to my parents' home since moving to Narragansett — and both of the previous visits had lasted for less than twelve hours. No sleepovers, no late-night talks that would end with me explaining again why I refused to leave my small fishing town. They couldn't hear me. Just like I couldn't hear them when they'd plead their case to move back to New York, to reapply to film school, to reapply to a different school, to get my life back on track. On track was a very big thing for them — almost as big as leaving Rhode Island in the first place.

And leaving Rhode Island in the first place was something I certainly wasn't intending to do anytime soon. I felt too safe there. No one expected anything of me, no one expected me to take any chances. Which was a good thing, as I felt ill-equipped to take any.

It seemed like the norm in Narragansett to put your life on hold — so many of the wives always talking to me about what they would do if (and only if) they could get out of town, how differently they would live *then*. Like Sue #2, for example — she'd always wanted to move to Montana; Nicole #4 — Michigan; Theresa #1 — Nevada; Beth #3 — Arizona. But always somewhere landlocked, always somewhere opposite, as if the opposite held the answer.

Still, my lack of return trips home bordered on unmanageable for my parents, especially for my mother, even with her daily phone calls to me. And they were, always, daily. But she too slowly began acquiescing to our biweekly dinners somewhere in the middle, usually Hartford or Westport. It was just smarter that way. It made it easier for all of us that way to pretend our real lives weren't so far apart.

I would never admit it out loud, but I did miss coming home. As hard as Scarsdale sometimes was for me, growing up, I'd always loved everything about my family's actual house: my bedroom exactly as it had been since my twelfth birthday — a grown-up room for back then — no flowery wallpaper or purple carpet. Just soft yellow walls, wide-circle throw rugs and picture frames, long gold silk on the windowsills. The windows themselves were a stainless glass that looked out over the backyard, the hilly enterprise of it, separate from the rest of the house.

The first floor was just one large window-filled room, everything swimming into everything else: living area, dining room, kitchen. Sun area nook.

Then there was the wraparound porch. It was the first thing you'd see when you walked up the front walkway: the large evergreens and small potted flowers, the long pillowed bench running the length of the porch. As Josh and I headed toward it, I saw that someone was lying on it — the bench — a familiar someone. Jaime Daniel Berringer. Josh's best friend since before I was born. Long and lanky, with a pile of blond floppy hair on his head. Little-boy good-looking in a way that stops you until you know him. Then it stops stopping you.

And like a million times before, there he was, just lying there on his back, his eyes closed, a bowl of cereal on his chest. Berringer always had a bowl of cereal on his chest — his food of choice for as long as I'd known him — a fact that was particularly bizarre, considering that he was now the chef at a nationally renowned French restaurant right outside of San Francisco.

Josh and I stood in the doorway, staring down at him. "You think that he's sleeping?" I whispered.

Berringer started to smile, but then tried to hide it, continuing to lie there, pretending to sleep.

Josh put his finger to his lips, motioning for me to play along.

"He must be," he said, as I tiptoed over to the bench, starting to sit down gently on the bench's edge. But just as I made my final move — my face right on top of his, my chest above his chest — Berringer sat up a little too quickly, banging into me. Forehead first.

"Ow!" I said.

"Ow yourself," he said, rubbing his head, laughing. His smile was so big now, it took up his entire face.

Somehow, he had saved his cereal.

This was when he first really looked up at me, his smile gone. "Emmy," he said, holding his hand to his chest, the one that had just been on his forehead. "Wow."

I touched my face, wondering if there was ketchup there, grape Popsicle stain. Josh certainly wouldn't have noticed and told me. "What? Do I have something?" I asked.

He sat back, moving farther from me, pulling his knees toward him. "Not at all. You just . . . you look so different."

I felt that in my chest. That he meant it. It had been years since we'd seen each other — since before I'd ended up in Rhode Island. I knew I looked different than I had then. I had slimmed down a little, and I let my hair grow out, learning slowly to leave it alone, letting it curl up the way it wanted. I was tanner, too, not quite so breakable-looking. I couldn't help it — I started to blush. But before I could say thank you, he interrupted me.

"You really look your age," he said.

"I really look *my age?*"

"Yeah," he said, touching the lines around my eyes gingerly. Then, as if remembering something, he turned and looked at Josh. "Josh, if your little sister's looking so ancient, how old does that make us?"

I slapped his hand away. "Thanks, Berringer," I said. "That's so nice of you to say."

Josh started to laugh. He was sitting on the ground across from us, leaning against the window. I looked over at him and then back at Berringer, who was also laughing now, his ear-to-ear smile back in full effect.

"Whatever," I said, standing up.

"Emmy, c'mon," Josh said. "He's just kidding around with you. He didn't mean anything by it."

"Honestly," Berringer said. "You look good. You know you do. I barely recognized you."

I guess this was supposed to be nicer. "I really don't care, Berringer," I said, even though I did, a little. He must have known it too. I'd had a huge crush on Berringer most of the time that I was growing up, right through my last year of junior high, right until he headed off to college. I remember trying to keep my mouth closed when I saw him, covering my braces, as if they were the problem. I tried to dress the way the older girls dressed. I kept my hair down. I used to daydream that he'd come home from school and see how different I was. Decide I was old enough. Now, I wasn't even sure he was.

I made my way to the front door, opening it quickly.

"So what's this I hear about a tackle shop?" he called out, stopping me. "You like fishing now?"

Instead of answering, I looked down at

Josh, who wouldn't meet my eyes. I wanted to say that I wasn't *only* working at a tackle shop, but who knew what my brother had told him? If Josh had mentioned that I was working on a documentary, which I seriously doubted, I was certain he didn't explain anything real about it, anything positive, like what I was hoping to learn about the wives, like what I was trying to accomplish. I wasn't about to get into that all now, especially considering that I hadn't yet. Learned anything. Accomplished anything.

I turned back to Berringer. "You know," I said, "this is not an ideal moment to make fun of me."

"I'm not making fun of you," he said seriously. "I'm curious to hear what you're up to."

I stayed fast in my position in the front doorway anyway. "Well, could you be curious a little later, please? I need to go inside and check on my mom."

"You might want to wait on that," he said.

"What are you talking about?" Josh said.

"The Moynihan-Richardses are in the basement," he said.

Josh sat up taller, his face turning worried — wrong — before my eyes. The Moynihan-Richardses were Meryl's birth

59

parents. The Ozark professors. The weirdos. From the back, they each looked more like how you might imagine the other looking: Dr. Moynihan-Richards with a long ponytail, wiry legs, Mrs. M-R with short, cropped hair and a black leather jacket that she never seemed to take off.

Under the best of circumstances, which these certainly weren't, the two of them staying here was a weird thing.

Berringer shrugged. "There was some sort of issue with them parking their RV near Meryl's parents' place in the city. It was like three hundred bucks to put it in the garage for the weekend or something crazy. So they showed up here about twenty minutes before you guys did. Your mom's in a bit of a tizzy."

He sounded so apologetic when he said the last part that I wondered if he knew that something else was going on with Josh. I bet he did. I bet he knew a lot more than I did. Like Elizabeth's last name. And where she lived. And what might happen next.

I looked over at Josh, who was starting to stand up. I quickly waved him back down. "I'll find out what's going on," I said, meeting his troubled glance, trying to calm him. "Just stay out here."

"You sure?" he said.

"Positive," I said, opening the door. I looked at Berringer, who was looking at Josh with so much concern that I immediately forgave him for his age joke. I'd immediately forgive him everything, if he could somehow just make this okay again. "You want a beer, Berringer?" I asked him.

He turned back toward me, giving me a smile. "You don't have to do that," he said.

"I know I don't have to."

He smiled. "I'd love one then."

I smiled back at him, tapping on the doorframe, before walking into the front hall. Maybe this would be okay. Maybe Josh would talk to Berringer and they'd work it all out, the confusion or hesitation or whatever you wanted to call it that Josh seemed to be feeling. Maybe Berringer would know, better than me, the right thing to say to calm him down.

Only I didn't close the door completely, and unfortunately, I was able to hear Josh's next question.

"Meryl didn't come with them, did she?" he said.

Berringer said, "Not that I saw."

This was when my brother, sounding not at all like himself for the second time that night, said: "Well, thank God for that, at least."

The thing I was starting to learn about wedding weekends was that they encourage people to revisit the past. Isn't that what wedding toasts are all about, really? This bringing to the surface of all the old stories, the private anecdotes, that we want to relive in order to feel like we all really know somebody — feel reinforced as to who they are — so we can let them go? Even before the actual wedding, even over the course of a wedding weekend, you can start to see this freshly minted need to disclose — everyone talking to each other a little differently, more honestly.

One of my mother's favorite stories, which I knew would come up before any future wedding of mine — and probably in some capacity over the course of Josh and Meryl's wedding also — was of the time that I asked her to marry me. I was maybe seven. Halfway through first grade. And when I asked her, she told me no. She gently explained that she couldn't marry me because she was my mother, to which I apparently responded, "Then I'll marry Daddy." Getting the same answer on that end — *You can't marry your father because he's your father* — I said with great reluctance that I would marry Josh. And when she told me there would be no dice on that end either, I had the first of several complete breakdowns. 'You mean to tell me that I'm going to grow up one day, and have to marry a *complete* stranger?'

As many times as I'd heard it, I actually always looked forward to this story because it reminded me about what I've always loved most about my mom. (Aka Sadie Meredith Everett. Born 1949, Reading, CT. Steadfast Virgo. Former schoolteacher.)

Sadie's favorite part of the story wasn't — nor had it ever been — the arguably cute moment at the end when I said that I didn't want to marry the stranger. It was the beginning.

When I picked her first.

I found my mother now in the kitchen, standing at the kitchen counter in her silk robe, fixing a ridiculously large platter of fruits and cheeses and crackers. She didn't look up at first when I walked in, which gave me a chance to watch her: her hair pulled back, sharp cheekbones, little elbows. I walked up behind her and put my hands on her shoulders. She was so little, my mother, much smaller than me, finer, with bones as tiny as pearls. It didn't seem to matter how many times I did it. It still scared me when I touched her.

"They're sleeping in sleeping bags down there," she said. "They won't even take my blankets. I can't even talk about it."

"We don't have to talk about it," I said into her shoulder.

"But don't you think that's bizarre?" she said, turning and looking at me — wild-eyed, devastated. "He doesn't even let her talk, really. He looks at her like she's crazy when she opens her mouth."

"What does that have to do with your blankets?"

"I think she wanted one."

I gave her shoulders a final squeeze and walked around to the other side of the counter, leaning up against it. I kept watching her. I was worried that she was going to ask me how the fireworks were. Knowing, if she did, she would hear too much of the real answer in my voice.

"What's going on?" she said, looking up. "I feel your eyes."

64

"You don't feel anything," I said, too quickly, and with a little more force than necessary. What else was I going to say, though? *I'm looking at you like this because out of nowhere, actually, Josh told me he might be in love with someone I'd never even heard of before tonight. Interesting turn of events, no?*

She looked at me for another second before returning to her cutting, unconvinced. "I know when I feel eyes," she said.

I shook my head no, and tried to figure out how to change the subject. The first thing I could think of was my documentary — the entirety of my fishermen's wives footage, all 107 interviews on thirty mini-DV tapes, sitting in the trunk of my car. I had run back into my house at the last minute that morning — pre–tackle shop — gathering the videotapes up to bring them home with me. This was due to a fleeting fear that the Narragansett house would burn down in my absence, the only copies of all of my research going up in flames. It was a baseless fear. I knew that somewhere inside. Except that I hadn't *not* slept in that house for so long that part of me did believe it was actually possible it would self-destruct in my absence.

"You know, I brought the fishermen's

wives footage home with me. To show you guys," I said quickly, before I could change my mind.

Maybe this wouldn't be the worst thing — showing the tapes to my family. Maybe when they watched it, they would think the footage was brilliant. And they could explain to me what I was missing.

"Not tonight, Em," she said. "Dad's already at the bachelor party."

"He's what?"

She shrugged. "He just thought someone needed to be there to welcome everyone," she said. "And you two didn't exactly seem to be doing great on timing tonight."

This was true. But I hadn't even known my dad was planning on going to the bachelor party in the first place. It was hard to picture him holding down the bachelor party fort, casually ordering drinks and making small talk with Josh's friends. I pictured him calling home every few minutes to ask my mother what he was supposed to do next.

"You know," my mom said, keeping her eyes averted, "you *did* have a visitor earlier this evening. He was very disappointed to have missed you."

"What are you talking about?" I said. I

couldn't imagine who would have come by to see me. I couldn't even think of anyone I had told that I was coming home. I hadn't told anybody. I knew I hadn't. Because I didn't *talk* to anybody from home — the entirety of my exchanges with friends from high school were exceedingly limited since I dropped out of a life I thought they could recognize. It wasn't that they all were becoming doctors and lawyers and bankers — though many of them were. It was more that they were becoming something. And I — one fragmentary interview at a time — wasn't.

My mom put down her knife in a grand gesture of emphasis. "I'm talking about Justin Silverman," she said. *"Justin Silverman!"*

Justin Silverman and I had "gone out" in junior high before either of us was allowed to go out anywhere without our parents. "I don't understand," my mother loved saying back then, "how are you going out with someone you never go anywhere with?" If she didn't dial down her excitement level, I was going to have to remind her of that.

"Justin Silverman came by?" I said. "To see me?"

"Well, Justin Silverman's mom," she said. "But the point is, Justin just graduated at the very top of his class from Northwestern Law School, and he's back in New York now! Is that not so exciting?"

Here we went. This was the first of what I knew would be many attempts by my mother to remind me, over the next couple of days, of the many opportunities in New York — men, jobs, hope — all the things that I was giving up in my makeshift life too far from home.

"It's so exciting, what he's doing. All this work with intellectual property. You know who would be totally interested in all the work he's doing with intellectual property? *You.* Which is why I told Evelyn to bring him by the rehearsal dinner tomorrow night so the two of you could catch up."

"What? Mom, why on earth would you do that?"

"Emmy. *Because.* Justin's back in New York now."

"Does he know I'm not back in New York now?"

She put the apple down, looking up at me. "What can it possibly hurt to spend five minutes with an old friend? Evelyn says he's gotten very handsome."

"Evelyn is his mother."

"So shouldn't she know?"

I crossed my hands over my chest, in

amazement at this standoff. There was not — and never had been — a way to argue with my mom. At least not one that I had found. And before I could even *not* attempt to this time, Josh walked into the kitchen, coming up behind our mom.

He put his hands on her shoulders, the same way I had moments before, and leaned in to give her a kiss hello on the cheek. "You okay?" he asked.

She shrugged, giving off a little sigh. But then she turned and actually looked up at him, and a smile started growing on her face. He matched her smile — the same half-baked expression they each were prone to wearing — an undeniable reminder of how alike they looked: same baby nose, hazel eyes. Same skin. Watching them, from my side of the counter, I had the feeling I used to have when I was little — that she must love him more because he looked so much more like her than I did. Now, though, that feeling held relief in it instead of the opposite.

Berringer appeared in the kitchen doorway, his T-shirt wrinkled from his fake nap, his dolphin boxer shorts sneaking out from beneath the top of his jeans.

I wanted to reach out and touch them.

My mom looked over at him, wiping her

hands on her robe. "Jaime here really saved the day with everything," she said. "They probably would have slept in the RV if it weren't for you."

He smiled. "You just got to know how to talk to people," he said.

"Is that what you've got to know?" I said, meeting his eyes. He looked back at me, but didn't say anything.

Josh looked back and forth between us, and announced that it was probably time to go, unless someone thought he should go and say hello to his future in-laws in the basement.

"They're probably sleeping now," my mom said, shaking her head. Then she looked down at the platter of food, arranged decoratively in several half-moons.

Before anyone could comment, she said, "There's a mini-fridge down there, remember?" No one said anything. "I can't talk about it."

Josh laughed, and then motioned toward me. "You ready to get out of here?" he asked.

For a second, I thought I'd misheard him. I was sure of it actually. "What are you talking about?" I said. "I'm not a bachelor."

My mom pointed at me. "You're not

married either," she said.

I turned back to Josh, confused. While I had helped with the b-party planning, I had never intended on actually attending. I intended on being in my childhood bedroom — sleeping — and getting a hungover thank-you from Josh tomorrow morning for sending out a very nice e-mail invite.

"Look," he said, "it's not like there's a team of strippers you'll be interrupting. I want you there."

When Josh was a teenager, he hadn't wanted me anywhere for a long time, the entirety of our conversations from the time he turned fourteen until he left for college occurring from either side of his closed door. I was always standing there, longingly, hoping he'd decide that day to let me in. It still surprised me more often than not how much he seemed to want me around now.

Berringer said, "I'm driving."

I started to follow them out of the kitchen, but before I could, Mom reached out to hold me back for a minute. Once their footsteps receded, she pulled me toward her and kissed my cheek.

"You are just the most beautiful in the world. You know that?" she said, stepping back and looking at me, smiling. Then she started pushing my hair back behind my ears, trying hard to flatten it down, make it stay.

"There," she said. "Much better."

That first summer after Matt and I were together, we planned a trip to Europe — a trip my mother pretended wasn't happening until after we'd already gone. It had been my first time leaving the country, my first time ever stepping foot off the continent. Every summer before that, I'd taken these nonnegotiable "Everett family road trips" to a different locale somewhere in America — Philadelphia, Virginia Beach, Wyoming. Always by car, always somewhere we could drive to, even if the drive took the better part of a week.

The one — and only — time my parents had let me decide on our family's destination, I chose London. I couldn't have been more than seven or eight. But even when my father tried to show me on our map-of-the-world chessboard that Europe wasn't drivable — wasn't even in the United States — I wouldn't pick somewhere else. I flat-out refused, and told him he should just let Josh pick instead. I told him I hated chess anyway.

Which meant that going to Europe, especially with Matt, meant a lot to me. I think my mom was comforted somewhat that during the France leg of the trip, I was going to be staying with Berringer — *we* were going to be staying with Berringer — who was living in Paris that year. He was taking some courses at the Culinary Institute, and apprenticing in a fancy hotel kitchen.

Only, when we arrived at his apartment, he wasn't there. He'd left a note that he had to go with his girlfriend to see her parents in England, but make ourselves at home and help ourselves to whatever we needed and there was cereal in the cupboard.

What I didn't know at the time was that the reason Berringer had gone with his girlfriend — Naomi, a British girl — to see her parents was that he'd asked her to marry him, and they'd gone together to tell them. Naomi was ten years older than Berringer and absolutely striking: long red hair, winter skin, thin fingers. She'd come into the fancy hotel restaurant for dinner — that was how they met — and, the way the story went, Berringer asked her to marry him that very first night, in the alley outside. This wasn't confirmed for me until their actual wedding ceremony the next December — when it was confirmed, again and again, usually along with the expression: *When you know, you just know.*

The wedding took place in Katonah, a quiet town thirty miles north of Scarsdale, at an inn on a farm. It was a small wedding, but my whole family went. I hadn't wanted to go because I was in the middle of finals. "Since when do you study?" my mom had asked. It wasn't a bad point. Josh was the best man and had to read this long poem about roses. Beautiful Naomi wore no shoes.

Now I stared at Berringer's reflection in the rearview mirror, his eyes hard on the road and both hands on the wheel, and I wondered, with Josh's looming nuptials, if Berringer was thinking about Naomi, if he still often thought about Naomi. They'd moved to New York after that year in Paris when Berringer got an assistant chef position at a new restaurant on the Lower East Side. And it was three years later, closer to four actually, that Naomi asked him to quit and find a job in London instead because she was homesick. Because she wanted to go home again.

But less than a week after they arrived in

London, she woke up next to him in their new apartment and said that it turned out she hadn't been homesick after all — she just didn't want to be married anymore.

That was the last I heard about Berringer for a long time. He disappeared into the recesses of northern California by way of Santa Fe, New Mexico, by way of Austin, Texas. Josh would give me updates occasionally, but I was too wrapped up in my own thing to pay good attention. That same summer, the one that Naomi asked Berringer to leave, was the one that Matt asked me to marry him. It was the day after my college graduation — a few days after Matt finished his first year of architecture school — and we were driving down south to spend a couple of days with my father's family in Savannah. We spent the first night camping right outside of Charlottesville, Virginia, and, right before we fell asleep, we thought we heard a bear outside the tent, rummaging through the trash. It turned out be a raccoon that — through a mix of shadows and strange moonlight and too much dinner tequila — seemed bigger than he was. And when we figured out what was really going on and stopped laughing, Matt asked me. Right then. In the midst of the imaginary bear.

He just pulled the ring out of his bag and said he didn't want to wait for the special dinner he had planned for us in Savannah. That he didn't want to wait. Did Berringer even know that? I doubted it.

I doubted that Berringer knew the first time Matt and I talked about marriage seriously was all those years before while staying at his apartment in Paris. That that very first morning we were there, we had gone to see the Eiffel Tower, and that was when he brought it up. He had said he could imagine the two of us taking a lifetime of seeing places like this — wanted a lifetime of that — that the best part of being in France was seeing how happy it was making me. I started crying, right beneath the Eiffel Tower. Because I knew he meant it, and it was how I felt about him — how I'd felt since the minute I met him — the best part of *everything* was watching him enjoy it too.

Part of me wanted to tell Berringer that story now, though I wasn't sure why. I wasn't sure what I thought that was going to do.

"Do you guys know anyone who is in a happy marriage?" I asked instead, sitting up taller. "A really happy one?"

Josh turned around and looked at me

from the front seat. Berringer met my eyes in the rearview mirror.

"I was just thinking," I said.

Josh turned back around, away from me. "Well, think about something else."

I looked into the rearview mirror to see if Berringer was still looking back at me. He wasn't. His eyes were back on the road. Now I knew he was thinking about Naomi. Naomi, and maybe his new girlfriend — Cecilia or Chloe, I forgot — something with a C. Carol Ann, maybe.

"Sorry, I was trying to figure something out about when things go wrong . . . between two people." I shook my head, knowing I wasn't making anything any clearer. For them or me. "Forget it. It was a dumb question," I said.

"Not for the back of a slam book, maybe," Josh said.

"Wow," I said. "I loved slam books."

Berringer met my eyes in the rearview mirror, again, and started smiling. "Favorite song? Not now, of course. Then."

I shook my head, trying to think of it, to remember, truly, what I had loved in sixth grade, in seventh, my pen crossing neatly in someone else's keepsake — me absolutely sure of my answers. " 'Lady in Red,' I guess," I said.

" 'Lady in Red,' " Josh mumbled under his breath.

"Favorite hobby?" Berringer asked, ignoring him.

"Taking baths," I said.

"Taking baths?" Josh said. This time he turned all the way around to face me. "Please tell me that you didn't actually used to write that down. What's wrong with saying softball? Or ballet?"

"I used to pretend it was the ocean," I said.

"That's great, Emmy," he said. "That's really great."

"I like taking baths," Berringer said.

Josh put up his hand to silence him. He couldn't take it when he thought I was being weird — not because he was embarrassed so much, but more because it made him worry about me. It made him worry that I'd get into a situation one day he couldn't get me out of.

He rolled down the window, the air hitting me, maybe even more than it was hitting him. "Now that you live near the ocean," he said, "maybe you can pretend it's a bath."

If you were coming to Scarsdale to visit someone — a roommate from college, say, or a new boyfriend's parents — and someone suggested going to get a drink, the odds were the next suggestion would be heading over to the Heathcote Tavern. The reason for this was that the Heathcote Tavern was the only place to go. I don't mean only as in the hip place, or the happening one. I mean only as in one and only. If you wanted to go to another bar, you'd have to head to another town. Like White Plains, maybe, or the main drag in New Rochelle.

The tavern wasn't a bad place, though. I'm not saying that. It was, actually, pretty great: three big, red rooms with fireplaces and dim lighting and dark wallpaper. Downstairs dining area. And upstairs was the bar itself — a space that was beyond crowded two nights a year, Christmas Eve and Thanksgiving Eve, when most SHS graduates from the last decade made their way back to town for the holidays and staged impromptu, unofficial reunions at the only place they could.

The rest of the year though, like tonight, there was usually only a smattering of people populating the upstairs bar late-night: a divorced couple on some sort of first date in the corner, an older man talking to the bartender by the flat-screen television, a couple of late-twenty-something women — their backs to us — drinking chardonnay at the bar.

Of course, tonight, for Josh's shindig, there was the addition of a long oval table in the center of the upstairs room reserved for and composed of Josh's relatively weak-looking bachelor party. On one side of the oval were Josh's other friends from high school — Mark, Todd, Chris — all of whom I recognized. On the other was the college and medical school representation, most of whom I didn't. Almost everyone had carpooled here from the city, where they either lived or were staying for the weekend at the Essex House, courtesy of Meryl's mom. When I saw the sheer number of empty shot glasses on the table, I realized this was a mistake. Having the bachelor party out here. At the rate everyone seemed to already be going, they'd be joining the Moynihan-Richardses in our basement.

When Josh walked up the stairs, someone called out, "There he is!" and everyone stood up and clapped, continuing with cheers as he went around the table saying hello. Berringer and I stood off to the side.

And I would have kept standing to the side, except I was noticed by my father, who at the head of the table was holding center court. He saluted me, and I saluted back. Samuel Bean Everett, Esq.: volunteer firefighter, Savannah, Georgia, native, six-foot-four anomaly. He had come tonight fully bachelor-partied out in construction pants, work boots, and a T-shirt Josh had bought him a few years back that read MR. SMOOTH LIVES HERE in large black letters.

Even from several feet away, I could see that tonight's festivities were affecting him. His cheeks were already red, his eyes watery. My dad rarely drank — a by-product, I always assumed, of being married to Sadie the teetotaler. I hadn't known my mother to have a drink, in fact, even once over the span of my lifetime. This was a little ironic when you considered that she met my dad at a bar. On a Sunday morning, nevertheless.

It was one of the stories that made the rounds — over and over — wedding weekend or not. The story of that New Year's Day morning spent at the Oak Bar — on the bottom floor of the New York Plaza. My mom and her friend Lydia were sitting at a corner table, drinking Shirley Temples. It had been Lydia's idea to go there as a way to kill a little time before the matinee they were seeing that afternoon. Enter my father. He had forgotten his newspaper at that very table, and was racing across the woody room to retrieve it. This was when she spotted him wearing "ripped dungarees" and his hair in a short ponytail. He was just passing through New York on his way from his home in Savannah, Georgia, to an island off the coast of Maine, where he was going to be a firefighter and coach high school basketball. He asked her to reach under the table and hand his paper back to him.

And in response, my mother, in an act that she maintains was completely unlike her, asked him to sit back down for just a minute and join them for another Shirley Temple. This baby-faced guy, who was pale-skinned and very southern and bright-blue-eyed, and who called her miss when he asked for his paper back and who wasn't anything like the guy that she thought she'd end up with: not wealthy or ambitious or Jewish. Not even Jewish.

While they were waiting for his drink to arrive — the story goes — she excused herself and went into the bathroom and locked herself in a stall and cried because she knew she'd never be okay without him.

Then she washed her face and checked her reflection in the mirror and went back outside and asked him to stay with her in New York and reconsider what he wanted to do with his life and let her raise the children the religion she needed to and marry her one day. Or, just to stay.

"Emmy!" My father screamed to me now. "What are you doing over there? Come over here. I want to kiss you hello, little beauty."

I hated when he called me little beauty. How had he turned out six-four, and his only daughter five-three? I looked at Berringer to see if he heard, but he was wrapped up in a conversation with the high school boys and had forgotten all about me.

I headed over to my father. "What's going on?" I said, as he leaned down and gave me a hug hello.

83

He pointed to his shirt. "The guys nick-named me Mr. Smooth. Isn't that something?"

"It's something," I said.

He looked down at his shirt, running his finger along the MR. SMOOTH. "It is something."

I delivered my mother's brief message that she was going to bed, and he looked up at me, more than a little worried at what I'd said, like he had maybe done something wrong, which he hadn't. It was just that they were rarely apart. That was the thing about my parents. They were still so much in love. Thirty-plus years later. They remained the only answer I had to the question I had asked Josh and Berringer in the car. Who was happily married? Who still loved each other? The problem was that with your parents, it sometimes seems like it doesn't count.

"Does she want me to come home?"

"Nope. She said, Just tell Dad I'm going to feed the Moynihan-Richardses and then pretend to go to sleep. Honest. All's quiet on the western front.' "

More convinced than before, he rubbed his hands together, relieved. "Then how about another round?" He turned toward everyone, talking more loudly, almost screaming, really. "How about another round, boys?"

He started walking toward the bar, but then he tripped, knocking two beers right off the table.

"Whoa there, Mr. Smooth," I said, trying to sit him back down. "Let me get it, okay?"

"Thank you, baby. I'm not used to drinking," he said, reaching up and touching my cheek. His palm was warm and wet from the alcohol. "You happy tonight?" he asked.

"I'm happy tonight."

He looked at me, trying to consider if that were true, trying not to act like he was considering. He had this small fear — my father — inherited from my mother's Jewish worriedness, that if I weren't completely okay, he had failed me.

He was the same way with Josh, which was how I knew what was coming next. He looked over to where Josh was standing, talking to a friend from medical school. Josh was clenching and unclenching his left hand, laughing. I guess they were joking around about the ring that was going to be there soon enough. I guess they were joking about everything that was coming next.

My father was smiling at him, like he'd received the information he needed. I was tempted to tell him the truth — that it was looking like it was turning out to be, at the very least, a little more complicated than that.

But I knew our dad wouldn't be able to handle that. He was the ultimate people-pleaser. That was where Josh got it from. The only instinct in him that even began to rival the people-pleasing gene was the overprotective one for Josh and me. If he had to handle this situation, the two sides of him would be forced to go head to head, and I worried he'd combust. I wasn't ready to watch that.

"They're going to be really happy, don't you think so? Meryl and Josh, I mean," he said, turning back to face me. "Don't you think Meryl's going to make him happy?"

I touched the top of his head. "Probably," I said.

Clearly I hadn't been paying very good attention to what was going on elsewhere at the tavern, but I still couldn't believe that I had failed to notice that I knew, all too well, the two twenty-something women drinking chardonnay at the bar. How could I not tell from the back of their heads?

Those two perfectly straightened heads. I should have at least recognized that I recognized them. But it took coming up right next to them at the bar, actually, to realize that they were none other than Stacey Morgan and her sidekick, Sheila Beth Gold: two girls I'd graduated high school with, still best friends apparently, and even prettier and more put together than they had been a decade ago. At one point, in high school, I could have almost been considered friends with them. We went to the same parties, hung out with the same group of guys, sat at lunch tables *near* each other in the back of the cafeteria. But now it was like they were donning bright HAZARD signs — ready to announce exactly where they were on their road from Superwoman City Girl to Soccer Momdom. Even if I were still with Matt, they would have thought my "film dreams" were just a quirk that would one day pass. And now that I didn't even have Matt as a common ground, well, I wasn't counting on the never-ending fishermen's wives project to win me any admiration.

Before they saw me, I tried to back away undetected, but — as seemed to be turning into the theme of the night — it was too late.

"Oh, my God, Emmy Everett!" Stacey said. She reached for my arm. She reached for my arm and held on. "Sheila, look! Emmy freaking Everett. I don't believe it. How are you, girly?"

"Hey, Stacey," I said, leaning in and patting her shoulder. It was an awkward move — not quite a hug, not quite not a hug. It was worse than if I hadn't done anything at all. "Sheila," I said.

"What are you doing here?" they said in unison.

I smiled, taking advantage of the time it gave me to try to mobilize my inner troops. I could get in and out of this conversation unharmed. Of course I could. I just needed to keep moving.

"Oh, it's actually a bachelor party for my brother," I said.

"Oh, that's right!" Stacey said. "Josh is getting married this weekend, isn't he? I knew that. I think my mom told me." She looked past me, to him, at the table. "You think it's too late to tell him I had a huge crush on him when he was in high school?"

"Maybe not," I said.

She looked at me, confused, and then — trying to recover for her — Sheila gave me a big smile.

"Well," she said, "we were supposed to

be on our way to the Hamptons right now, but by the time we got going, traffic was just too awful. So we decided we'll spend the night in the 'dale and head out early tomorrow . . . we probably should have just taken a jitney right from Midtown instead of coming all the way out here to get the car."

"Well hindsight's twenty-twenty, right?" I said. "At least you'll have the car out at the beach."

"At least we'll have the car out at the beach," they echoed.

I motioned toward the bartender. "Could I get another round of tequila shots when you have a minute?" I asked. "And the rest of the bottle? The rest of the bottle would be great."

They waited for him to start rounding up the drinks before they continued, as if he cared what we were talking about, let alone wanted to listen. I didn't even want to listen, and I had no choice.

"So," Stacey said. "Last time we saw you, Miss Emmy, you were about to get married. You early bloomer! I mean, I always thought I wanted to be further along in my career before all of that, but the more crummy I'm-not-going-to-commit-to-you-while-there-is-even-one-modelat-Bungalow-8 guys I'm meeting in the city, the more I'm thinking I should have just settled early on like you did. Big deal if I'm the number-three girl for the number-two guy at the biggest litigation firm in New York? I want someone to brush my teeth with. What was the name of that television show that was on for two minutes where the blond girl said that? That she wanted someone to brush her teeth with? Anyway . . . I'm ranting. The point is, we want to hear *what you're up to.* What's your husband's name again? Matthew? He was studying to be an architect, right? You tell us. How is married life? With a fancy architect?"

Stacey took a deep breath in, which made me realize that I hadn't taken one either the entire time she'd been talking. I wished more than anything then that I was married to Matt, that I could give them a happy report. Especially because Stacey was beaming again, already smiling again so widely that I understood that even her problems didn't really bother her. She didn't *really* fear she wouldn't find someone. She didn't really fear. She was the number-three girl for the number-two guy at the biggest firm in New York City. This was just her opening statement of practiced misery. So I would end up saying something back that would reaffirm for her that she was in the best place she could be in, the only place, and she should feel good about it.

I pulled my hair tighter behind my ears, bracing myself. "Well, you know," I said, and shrugged, "you may want to ask someone who's actually married. That didn't end up happening for me."

"Jeez, Emmy, I'm sorry," Sheila said, reaching out and touching my wrist. "I'm really sorry."

I tried to wave it off. "That's okay," I said.

"Oh, of course it is. Of course!" Stacey said, Sheila nodding her head, fiercely, in agreement. "Things sometimes happen. Things change! The important thing is the present. What are you up to now, Emmy?"

"I'm working at a fishing supply store in Rhode Island," I said.

"Oh." They looked at each other. "Huh."

The bartender placed down the tray of tequila shots, the bottle sitting in the middle of the tray. I picked up the tray and then turned back to the girls, holding it up in their direction. "Well, I guess I should be getting these over to the table," I said.

"But don't worry. I'll be back in a minute to get everyone else's."

They looked at each other, again, and then both started laughing, a little too hard. But I guess that's what you get for offering up a bad joke, or, maybe, for seeming a little too much like one yourself.

When I got back to the table, my father was telling a story. I put the booze quietly in the center and sat down in the chair next to Berringer. He looked over at me and gave me a smile, and then turned his attention back to my father, whose arm was around Josh. I was only catching the tail end of the story, but I'd heard it before. It was the one when Josh was pitching his first junior varsity baseball game. Josh had been pitching a no-hitter until the last inning, when someone hit a home run out of the park. "Josh ran up to the home plate and broke the bat in half because he was so convinced the guy put cork inside," my father was saying.

Everyone laughed, except me. I was too busy wondering if all bachelor parties were this much fun.

Berringer leaned in toward me. "Are those friends of yours?" he asked, motioning to Stacey and Sheila at the bar.

I shrugged, reaching straight across him for a tequila shot. "Why do you ask?"

"You look upset."

I downed the shot, instead of answering him. Then I reached for another. I started to ask if he remembered Sheila and Stacey, mostly because I thought he wouldn't. Which I thought would make me feel better. But before I even could, he leaned forward and whispered in my ear.

"When I tell certain people that I'm a chef, they look at me funny, and ask what I like to cook," he said. "And I know if I say I like making some really fancy dish, like margret of duck with verjus, or whole roasted squab and truffles, or foie gras and anything, they'll approve. I know these are the things they want to hear."

"So what do you tell them?"

"Peanut butter," he said. "And jelly."

I started laughing, feeling a chill run through me, his lips still close to my ear, which I tried to ignore.

I pulled back and looked at him. "So, you want to tell me something, Berringer?"

He was still smiling at me. "Anything," he said.

"Have you met Elizabeth?" When he didn't answer, I tried to clarify for him. "Josh's Elizabeth."

"Emmy, you should probably be talking to Josh about this instead of me."

I motioned across the table to where Josh was taking another tequila shot of his own, quickly — his face starting to get red, a little too flushed. "Josh is busy right now," I said.

Berringer shook his head, keeping his eyes down. He certainly wasn't smiling anymore.

"What?" I said. "She's that great?"

He looked back up at me, reluctantly, offering a soft nod. "She's pretty great," he said.

I stared down at my empty shot glass, thinking of Meryl. She had just come to New York a couple of weeks ago for her final dress fitting, and had driven up to the Hilton in southern Connecticut to meet me for lunch. We ended up talking about this great documentary she had seen in L.A. about a filmmaker who was so in love with this old novel he read that he embarked on a countrywide journey to find the author, who hadn't been heard from in over two decades. She got so excited telling me the story that she decided we absolutely had to see it together *that* day, and we ended up driving another hour and half to this beautiful old theater in Northampton, Massachusetts — the only place it was playing anywhere in New England. It was the best day I could remember having in a long, long time. It would be the easiest thing in the world to make the argument that she was pretty great too.

"The point is, things shouldn't have gotten as far as they did with Elizabeth if he wasn't going to back it up," Berringer said. "Josh knows that. He knows it now. And wants to do the right thing here."

"The right thing for whom?" I said.

He didn't answer me, and I wanted to push it, ask him what that even meant — marrying Meryl or telling her the truth about Elizabeth? — but I wasn't sure Berringer knew the answer. I also wasn't sure that being right was as simple as I had been allowing for, as most of us allowed for, when we used it as an excuse to do what we thought we were supposed to do. Besides, what I wanted to ask Berringer more was which woman he thought Josh belonged with, and I knew he was never going to tell me that. He would say it wasn't his judgment to make. And maybe it wasn't. But I knew he had an idea anyway. He knew Josh better than anyone did — maybe even better than I did. He understood exactly what, in the end, he could and couldn't do. What maybe he needed to do.

"Elizabeth's a breeder," he said. "She breeds these enormous dogs, you know."

"Berringer," I said slowly, the beginning of the tequila making its way to my head. "I'm beginning to think I don't."

Apparently, their story went something like this.

That year — Josh's last of medical school, Meryl already in Los Angeles — Josh was volunteering a few times a month at a free clinic in Springfield, Massachusetts. There was a huge dog show in town at the Expo Center, which he wandered over to during his lunch break. Elizabeth was there, showing two of her dogs. Josh had told me a long time ago that he had this theory that an entire relationship was based on what occurred over the course of the first five minutes you know each other. That everything that came after those first minutes was just details being filled in. Meaning: you already knew how deep the love was, how instinctually you felt about someone. If one of you were saving the other at the beginning — like if you met during a car crash, for instance — you would continually take on that role (the

96

savior, the saved) in various capacities for the length of the union. Or: if you didn't inherently trust somebody, that, too, would be your gut reaction for as long as you knew each other, reaffirming itself beneath whatever good the other person tried to do for you.

"What happened in their first five minutes?" I asked Berringer now.

"Time stopped," he said.

Sometime around the real last call — not the one the bartender had quietly pushed back in honor of one *more* final round of drinks — my father stood up, clinked his spoon to his glass, and made a quick toast to Josh. No big stories, no teary eyes. Just a wish for him of true happiness. Josh was very red at this point, watching our father, and I could tell he was having trouble focusing on what was being said, but when our father was finished, Josh stood up and hugged him anyway.

"To the happiest weekend of your life," my father said. His voice all choked up, too thick.

"Oh, man, let's get out of here," I said, turning to Berringer.

I had already called a car service for the other guys. I had already made sure that was taken care of. Berringer nodded, but before we could stand up, my father was calling my name again, louder this time.

I looked up slowly, all eyes on me. "How about you?" He smiled, raised his glass. "You want to make a toast?"

Berringer caught my eye, not looking away. I tried looking around at this table of boys, none of whom I really knew. Not anymore. Then I looked at Josh. He was avoiding looking back. What did I know about him? All I could think was that he had this whole other life that he hadn't told me about until now. What else didn't I know about this person I really thought I knew everything about?

I had done all sorts of research on weddings in preparation for a toast. I had read a good half-dozen books on what different wedding rituals meant, where the traditions came from. I'd planned on incorporating all sorts of the bizarre trivia into whatever speech I ultimately made. But it didn't matter. For the life of me then, I couldn't think of one single thing to say.

"Come on, Em," my dad said. "Say something."

Josh smiled at me, winked. "She doesn't have to, Dad. Just drop it."

I tried to smile back at him, feeling

awful. Then I felt Berringer's hand on my back.

"You know what?" he said. "She was just telling me she's still doing some work on it. She's not wasting it on you guys."

I looked over at him gratefully — so gratefully, that it surprised me. It surprised both of us.

"She's saving it for the wedding," he said.

The Everett boys were drunk enough that we had to split them up for the car ride home: Josh slept in the back of Berringer's car, and I followed them, slowly, in our dad's. My dad was asleep as soon as he hit the passenger seat, before I even pulled out of the parking lot. Sneaking a peek at him, his mouth open — lightly snoring — I wished I'd sat tonight out, that he was in Berringer's car right now, and I had stayed at home to try to make some headway on the documentary. That I had stayed home and gone to sleep — so all of the things Josh had said would already be slipping away.

Behind me, someone honked. I looked in my rearview, the driver shining his brights at me, his red-right arrow. Which might be why instead of taking the requisite turn onto Heathcote Road — eventually leading to my parents' home on Drake — I headed straight toward Mamaroneck Road. No one behind me on the road, no one in front. I drove past the big church and the junior high, the run-down tennis courts. All the lights were out on the left except for one lone streetlamp, blipping on and off as if it were its only job.

I told myself I didn't know where I was going, but I did know. I knew as soon as I got to Cushman Road and took the familiar right, making the second turn onto Willow, pulling into the little cul-de-sac I knew by heart, circling the car around until I was facing the right backyard. It all looked the same from the back: three levels of colonial windows, the small attic perched on top, a rectangular backyard filled with swing sets and a slide and broken toys, all belonging to Matt's little brother.

I killed the ignition and sat back, taking a breath. There weren't any lights on in the house, not even the back porch light. And it occurred to me that Matt's parents were probably away for the Fourth — probably up at their home in Maine. It was possible that someone was home, and just sleeping. But I didn't think so. They were probably gone. And down the hall, Matt's room was probably empty.

We had spent so many afternoons in that

bedroom. I had spent so many afternoons there even without him, on the days he couldn't make it out to Scarsdale or I couldn't go into the city. It had made me calmer to be there among his things, doing my homework or wasting time. It was like he was there with me. Every Tuesday night my last year in high school, he'd come home and I'd stay there with him. That was our tradition — weekends together in the city, Tuesdays in Scarsdale. We'd get up at five in the morning, so we'd have a couple of hours together before I had to be at school: Matt bringing up a thin thermos of coffee from kitchen, that morning's paper, getting back into bed with me.

Part of me wanted to ring the bell now, or sneak in through the window, and just head back up to that room for a while. Not because it would make me feel any differently afterward, but because I wanted to feel again, for a few minutes, what it had been like. To belong to something bigger than myself.

He had had these thick sheets, this soft blue comforter. Why did the color matter to me? Why did I remember that? You can't really feel a color. You can't really feel anything entirely unless part of you doesn't know it's happening.

I shook my head, turning the ignition back on. I didn't need to be here. I didn't need to be anywhere but in my own bed, sleeping. Or knocking on the bedroom wall, seeing if Josh was awake and could hear me. If he wanted to talk.

My dad opened his eyes, abruptly, and turned toward me. But by then I was already pulling away.

"Is everything okay?" he asked.

"Everything's fine, Dad."

"Where are we?"

"Matt's," I said.

"Matt's?" He was confused, but his eyes were closing again. In a minute, I knew he'd be out.

"Well," I said. "Not anymore."

When we got back to the house, Berringer's car was still in the driveway. I carried my bags inside — fishermen's wives tapes included — and got a glass of ice water and left it on the floor by my father, who was passed out on the couch. Then I peeked in on Josh, just for a second, who was lying on top of his bedcovers, fully dressed, sleeping.

"This house is a mess," I said out loud, even though no one seemed to be sober enough to hear me.

I filled up another glass of water and went outside. I found Berringer out on the back steps, facing the yard. The tent was up for tomorrow already, these four six-foot-tall wooden lanterns firmly planted into the ground on every side. Berringer was looking out at all of it, an empty cereal bowl next to him.

I handed the water over. He smiled a thank-you at me, taking a huge sip, downing most of the glass, before he started speaking again. "I fear that the Everett men are going to be struggling a bit tomorrow," he said. "I left your dad a note on the kitchen table, telling him to have another beer in the morning. Hang-over cure. A hair of the dog that bit you."

I moved the bowl over, took a seat. It was still incredibly warm outside, the air thick and sticking to my skin.

I swirled the spoon around in the left-over milk. "What kind were they?" I said, motioning toward his cereal bowl.

"Honey Nut Cheerios." He said. "It's usually Honey Nut Cheerios at night."

"What about the morning?"

"Sometimes Special K. But mostly on Sundays."

I smiled at him, putting down the spoon. I could feel my heart beating in my head, my eyes starting to get heavy. "I'm not sure I should have been driving," I said. "Now that I'm sitting still."

"Yeah, well," he said. "I'm definitely walking home from here."

"In this heat?"

"It's going to be worse tomorrow."

"True," I said. "Isn't that a weird thing, though? That you can walk home. That our homes are still here? All this time after we left?"

"Well, our parents' homes."

"Still . . . I spend so much time trying to escape this place, and sometimes I wonder if it's the only place I'll ever have to really go back to. You know? If it's the only place I'll ever really consider home."

He handed me the glass of water. "Drink," he said.

I took the water from him, starting to laugh. He turned and looked at me, tilting his head. It was weird when he did that — looked at me from that direction. It was almost like he was trying to see something that I wasn't sure I wanted someone to see. It made me nervous.

"So." He smiled. "Tell me something more about this documentary of yours. You must be close to finishing by now, right?"

I felt something clutch inside. I didn't know what to say. I was used to explaining my life away with partial fictions, but it felt wrong, in a way I wasn't entirely used to, to tell him anything but the truth. Maybe because he seemed to have so little trouble telling the truth himself. What was I going to say anyway, though? That the more time I was spending on this documentary, the further away the end was becoming? That the more time I was spending, the less sure I was why I was doing it in the first place?

"Berringer, I think we have bigger things to talk about right now. Like Josh," I said. "Just for example."

"Ah . . . ," he said, nodding like he understood. "The girl swings it back to Josh when she doesn't want to talk about herself."

I ignored that, even though I knew, inside, he wasn't wrong. "I just don't understand," I said. "If you're saying Josh is so amazing with Elizabeth, that they have this amazing connection or whatever, why aren't you telling him? When it matters most that he does something about it?"

"It's past time for that. If he was going to do something, he should have done it already."

"What does that even mean?" I said.

"You want him to make a mistake?"

"Which way do you think is the mistake?"

I looked away, unsure of how to answer that. I had no answer. One minute I thought Josh should absolutely marry Meryl — that anything else would absolutely be the mistake — and then, in the next minute, I realized I didn't have enough information to know for certain. The only thing I did feel clear about — coming from my own personal experience of sitting absolutely still — was that Josh needed to do something, as opposed to just letting his life happen to him.

Berringer put his empty water glass down. "Maybe there's not a mistake to even make," he said.

I looked at him again, angry all of a sudden. Of course there was a mistake to make. There was always a mistake. I lived my whole life in the fear of making it. "Wasn't there one for you?" I said.

But as soon as the words were out, I was sorry, because I realized how cruel they sounded. And I knew they were really not directed at him at all, but more at myself. Or at Josh. Or someone else who didn't want to hear me.

"Berringer," I said. "I'm sorry. I'm just

getting frustrated because I can't get a handle on this whole thing. But I didn't mean that. I really didn't."

"Yes, you did, but that's okay," he said. He was looking at me now, but it was like he didn't see me.

Then he stood up. "Wait, you're going to leave over it?" I said. "I don't want you to leave over it."

He bent down and kissed me on the forehead, then bent even lower and I thought he was going to kiss me again, really kiss me — on my lips, my bottom lip — but he didn't. He just looked at me for a second.

"I'm not leaving over that," he said.

Then he was gone.

It was probably in large part because this wedding weekend was off to a lousy start that, after Berringer left, I just couldn't stop thinking about all the superstitious stuff surrounding weddings that I had been reading in planning Josh's toast: all these crazy dangers people used to face if they broke their commitment to marry someone, if they decided to do something else instead.

At one point people believed that if you were engaged more than one time, you were setting yourself up for damnation. Potential seventeenth-century grooms-to-be were so scared of this fate that they would look for certain signs before going ahead and proposing. In the days leading up to the proposal, seeing a monk on the street or a pregnant woman would predict a bad union. Seeing a pigeon apparently foreshadowed good things to come. These were rules, hard and fast, and people stuck to them. They gave you concrete ways to make decisions about whom to spend your life with. More concrete ways than how you felt or how you didn't feel at any given time.

Once you were engaged back then, that was as good as being married. If you broke your word on that — if you tried to get out of the engagement — that was going to lead you down a painful road. It was just as bad as divorce. It was sometimes considered worse.

What about now? Today? Did breaking off a commitment hold just as much terror? Even if society didn't condemn you in quite the same way as it used to, would you end up in a worse position than if — in spite of your doubts — you stuck to your original plan?

I started walking back up the stairs

slowly. Tomorrow was the rehearsal dinner. Less than forty-eight hours from now, the wedding was going to happen. Less than seventy-two hours from now, this would all be over. Meryl and Josh would be on their way to Hawaii and then back to Los Angeles, Berringer would be back in San Francisco, and I would be back in Rhode Island. That would be the end of all of this. No damnation for anyone.

So why then did I skip the entrance to my own bedroom? Why did I keep on walking, right into Josh's? I kept the door slightly ajar behind me, sliding slowly down to the floor by the closet. As my eyes adjusted to the dark, I could see that he was still lying on top of the covers, his arms over his eyes. I could see that he was now awake. I picked my words very carefully, knowing as I did that he would listen. Even if he didn't want to. He would listen to me.

"See, the thing is, Josh," I said. "I know why you told me about Elizabeth."

"Emmy," he said. "Do we have to do this right now? If I opened my eyes, I'd see seven of you."

I pulled my knees closer to my chest. "The reason is that you know I won't be able to let it go," I said. "Because, if the situation were reversed, you wouldn't let it go. Not until you knew I was okay."

Against the light coming in from the window, his chest rose up, fell again. I covered my eyes, my head spinning a little also. I wanted to finish this conversation. I wanted this to end, right here, okay.

"Are you okay?"

"Not really," he said.

I paused, but only for a second. "Do you think you need to see her?" I said. "Is that even possible?"

"She's in Pascoag."

I wasn't sure if that was a yes or a no.

"Pascoag, Rhode Island," he said. "It's on the northern tip. The other tip from you."

I didn't say anything. The northern tip was probably an hour from me, somewhere on the other side of Providence. I started doing the math in my head. If she were located north — that would take three hours at the least, probably closer to four. That would take the better part of tomorrow, just driving back and forth.

"It's a cool story, where the name Pascoag comes from. See, there's this cliff to the east of it, and getting over the cliff used to be the only way in to the town. But the problem was that the cliff was completely crawling with these snakes. Really enormous, boalike snakes. And you used to have to 'pass' all the snakes. So . . . pass coag."

I looked back down, shaking my head. I knew what was coming next, knew why he was telling me that story — knew he knew that I was a sucker for stories — knew even before I was willing to let myself admit that I knew it.

"It would really help if you would come with me, Emmy," he said finally.

"I'm not sure it would really help, Josh."

He put his hands over his eyes, already mostly asleep. "It would," he said.

I looked back down, my eyes starting to close too. If I were a different person, I could have slept right there. I could have bunched up a sweater under my head and wrapped my arms around myself and just drifted off. And then, maybe tomorrow, it wouldn't feel so pressing. Josh would submerge — the way he had been submerging — everything that was bubbling to the surface right now, everything he was too scared to be feeling.

For this reason, more than any other, I willed myself awake.

"Then," I said. "That's what we'll do."

part two

The week after Matt and I got engaged, my parents — in a notable act of engagement-present generosity — took us out for dinner and presented us with two plane tickets to Paris. I knew, of course, that my mom had picked Paris because when I'd returned from our first trip there some four years ago, I had told her all about how Matt and I had discussed getting married. And, more importantly, I had told her how excited I was about it, how I felt that something important had been solidified between us in Paris — something intangible, unnamable — that made me certain Matt was the person I was supposed to spend my life with, that made me certain, whatever my future held, he would be a part of it. And my mother had remembered, and wanted to celebrate that.

Only, on the cab ride back to our apartment after dinner that night, Matt asked me if I thought my parents would be offended if we exchanged the tickets for ones that would take us to another destination. Prague, maybe, or Vienna. "I just don't remember us having such a great time in Paris," he said. "You know what I mean? It wasn't so memorable."

What can I even say? There are moments when you can feel something fall down inside of you, and never rise up in exactly the same way again. For me, this was one of them.

"Women have better memories than men," he'd argued, when I tried to remind him of the conversation we'd had there about getting married, tried to relive for him that morning at the Eiffel Tower, that night in that small coffee-barroom, everything, *everything,* we had done together there, and that he'd seemed so excited about.

That was what I feared most: that he just wasn't excited about us anymore — that something between us had altered irreversibly. And afterward, I started seeing the evidence everywhere: in the way he didn't sleep facing me anymore, or the way he'd stopped asking me the questions he used to need to know the answers to, the way he stopped needing to tell me things in order

116

for them to count. At first I told myself I invented this. Or that I was overreacting. Especially because there were slight reprieves. He'd make us Valentine's Day dinner in bed, or leave a sunflower by the front door, he'd reach for my hand in the parking lot without looking first. But it was almost a sadder thing, waiting for these small victories. Because they were so infrequent, and because they seemed to be more like an apology for something he didn't have the strength to tell me about.

I waited it out anyway. I waited for almost a year, the entire length of our engagement, for Matt to show me someone resembling the Matt I thought I'd known. But the longer I waited, the more I understood that something crucial and irreplaceable had been lost, probably long before that cab ride when I first noticed its absence. Which left me with these constant questions — these awful, often avoidable questions — about what exactly I was willing to live without. In order to keep him. In order to not have to face the impossibility of another kind of life.

And now I couldn't help but worry about what kind of life Josh was walking into, or away from. Maybe it wasn't my job to figure it out, but it felt a little too close to home to not contemplate it, to not try to help him make some sense out of it. Better sense, at least, than I had managed to make of it for myself.

My alarm clock unsnoozed itself again, buzzing for the sixth time that morning, demanding that — whatever I thought — I at least did it fully awake. It was 6:34 a.m. We were supposed to be on the road fourteen minutes ago, and my head was still throbbing from my ample tequila consumption a few hours before. As if that wasn't grim enough, according to the thermometer that my father had put in the window sometime around my tenth birthday, it was already seventy degrees outside. Not even seven in the morning, and seventy degrees outside.

I flipped my alarm clock off and stood up.

"How is that possible?" I said, tapping on the thermometer, trying to regulate it. It held its ground.

"Who are you talking to?" Josh asked. He was standing in my doorway, dressed in jeans and a long-sleeved white shirt, a short-sleeved shirt with the word WORD on it over that. The car keys were already in his hands.

"You may want to change into something else." I pointed to the thermometer as my proof. "It's going to be a million degrees outside today."

"I'll take my chances," he said. "You ready?"

I was standing by my bed in the ripped T-shirt that I'd slept in, nothing on my feet, and it was all I could do not to ask, Do I look ready to you? But he was keeping his voice low, and I knew he was afraid we were going to wake our parents. So I just held up my hand to indicate that I needed another minute.

Josh nodded, disappearing down the hall, and I opened my closet, searching for the lightest pieces of clothing I could find. In lugging my fishermen's wives tapes inside, I had left behind all but a backpack of belongings in the car, figuring I'd just wear what I had in my closet this morning. It was a slim selection, to say the least. I settled on a yellow sundress, a pair of old flip-flops, and a beat-up cowboy hat.

I stood in front of the dresser mirror with the hat on, pulling my hair into two low pigtails. It wasn't a great look. My cheeks were still sallow from lack of sleep, my eyes too wide.

"I look like a little girl," I said to my reflection.

"You look fine," Josh said, appearing once again in the doorway, apparently out of nowhere.

"Stop doing that," I said.

"Doing what?"

"Materializing."

He motioned for me to follow him, and so I did, reaching for my pocketbook and then tracing his steps out of my bedroom and down the upstairs hallway, down the main stairs, out the front door. He didn't talk to me again until we were outside.

"I left Mom and Dad a note saying we were going to the city to spend the day with Meryl," he said, walking quickly. "I said that they could call your cell if they needed us for anything."

I tried to keep pace with him. "What did you tell Meryl?"

"What do you mean?"

"I mean where exactly did you tell Meryl you were going to be?"

"Meryl's going to be busy doing her own thing today," he said. "Everyone's in town. She has some sort of last-minute outing with Bess and the wedding planner."

By some strange twist of fate, Meryl had ended up hiring the same wedding planner I had been using to help plan Matt's and my wedding. Tiffany Tinsdale. Tiffany Tinsdale, who worked out of a townhouse on the Upper East Side, whose messiness she would apologize for — as soon as you walked in the door — knowing good and well the only thing ever out of place was the piece of paper she placed on the floor to pick up while she told you how sorry she was for the messiness. I thoroughly disliked Tiffany Tinsdale. And the feeling was mutual. She wanted me to care about all types of things I couldn't seem to care about at all: place settings, bridesmaid's dresses, party parting gifts. Those things didn't matter to me normally, and the way things were going with Matt, the wedding planning came to feel like an uncomfortable reminder that the wedding had become a show, a too-large production. And I didn't even know why I was putting it on anymore.

Tiffany. I could only be thankful now that there would be no visiting with her this weekend. When Meryl realized she had also worked on my nonwedding to Matt, she let Tiffany go and hired someone named Bethany instead.

I looked carefully at my brother. "So you're not worried?" I said. "That Meryl will be suspicious?"

"No," he said.

I kept looking at him, waiting for the rest

of it. I knew there was a rest of it because he was refusing to look back.

"I left her a voice mail that I'm spending the day with Berringer and to call his cell phone if she needs me, okay? And no, Emmy," he said, anticipating my next question, "I don't think I'll get caught."

This made me think. First that he was wrong, and he was going to get caught. And, then, that he wasn't wrong. That he had done this before, so many times by now, that he knew exactly how to manage it.

He clicked open the car doors, and I got into the passenger side, watched as he slid into the driver's seat.

"You know, I'm not sure I like you so much right now," I said once he closed the door.

"Well," he said, "if it's any consolation, I'm not sure I like myself."

The quickest way to Rhode Island from our parents' was to take 287 to I-95 and then just stay on it, straight, all the way along and through Connecticut, one long boring shot. If everything went as scheduled, this would land us on my edge of Rhode Island in a little over three hours, on Elizabeth's edge — I was guessing — fifty minutes or so after that.

When we hit 287, I rolled down my window and put my hand outside, the wind pressing up against it. I knew that things were supposed to look better in the morning, but I was still waiting for better to kick in. I was nervous about meeting Elizabeth, nervous I wasn't going to like her, and even more nervous that I would. And more than anything, the absurdity of this — the rush, rush of it — wasn't quieting what I felt just under the surface. That as soon as we stopped, there was going to be all kinds of unhappiness.

I was guessing that Josh felt it too. Because he was driving uncharacteristically slowly, cars speeding past us on the left: two matching green Saabs, an SUV, a minivan full of kids, who waved at us as their parents passed.

He waved back.

"Remember the time," he said, "when we drove all the way to Arizona for the summer trip? I think I was in seventh grade. So, what were you, in second? That was the last time we went that far."

"I'm pretty sure we went to Colorado after that," I said.

"Colorado's not as far as Arizona, Emmy."

"Oh."

He looked at me blankly. "Do you really not know that?"

"Josh!" I said. "Does this anecdote of yours have a point? Or do you want to critique my geography skills?"

"What geography skills?"

I gave him a look too, before fixing my gaze back out at the road. The little boy from the minivan was gesturing wildly at me and sticking his tongue out. I stuck mine out back.

"My point is," Josh said, "that I think it was in Arizona when you made up that game. You know, when you'd scream, Wolf! out the back of the window if you didn't recognize the car behind you? What was that game called?"

"Wolf."

"That's right. Wolf. Now, that was creative."

I rolled my eyes in disbelief that it had taken me this long to see it coming. But now I knew. I knew what was coming next — some version of Josh's you're-not-supposed-to-be-living-your-life-in-this-way speech. You're supposed to be doing something creative. You're supposed to be doing something.

"You know, Josh," I said, "I really don't think you're in a position to lecture me about anything right now."

"Who's lecturing? I'm not lecturing. I'm just saying."

I closed my eyes. "Well, wake me when you're done saying."

"You never want to talk about this, Emmy. How you're just, like, wasting more and more time away in Rhode Island. You never want to deal with it at all. Even Meryl says . . ."

I opened my eyes and looked at him. I couldn't believe he was bringing up Meryl now. How could he think that was a good idea? It was like he had totally lost any sense of reality.

I tried to stay calm. "Honestly," I said. "Why do you think you are entitled to make choices about my life? What qualifies you for that? The great ones you are making in your own?"

"That's mature," he said. "I'm a doctor."

I shook my head, turning away from him. I really didn't want to talk about any of this anymore. I understood that Josh didn't want me in Rhode Island — that he didn't want me doing what I was doing, or not doing. But the way I figured it, he was out of line getting so bent out of shape. I could do anything in Rhode Island that I could do in New York City. Or Los Angeles. Or anywhere else for that matter. And for all he knew, I was.

"Did you not see all of the tapes sitting in my bedroom?" I said. "Does the documentary I'm working on not count at all?"

"Right, the *documentary.*" His voice had an edge to it, which I tried my best to plow right through.

"It's just so fascinating, you know? These women have partners who spend more than half their time away from home. Four weeks, six weeks at a time . . . can you imagine what it must be like to be married to someone who is always going to leave you? What that must be like to be the one who is always waiting for someone to come back? Pretty interesting stuff to think about."

"Yeah, I've got to say," he said, "I don't really think it's such an original topic."

"Not so original?"

"Right."

I stared him down. "So, Wolf is genius, but taking a look at a difficult aspect of an understudied subculture's life isn't very creative?"

Before he could even attempt an answer, I put my hand up to silence him. It was enough, and quite honestly, I was feeling more than a little defensive about my documentary, somewhat troubled as it was. Of course, Josh couldn't understand its value. He'd never been waiting for anyone. He'd never been left. He was too busy keeping everyone in.

But the thing was, I wasn't exactly finding endless cohorts among the wives either. While a lot of them didn't like the separation from their husbands, many of them didn't necessarily talk about feeling abandoned or left behind, either. Maybe that was part of my documentary trouble. I wanted to hear that everyone did feel so badly, too. So I wouldn't feel as badly feeling that way myself. The more time that went by, though, the less I could deny it. As much as I was trying to make the wives fit the pattern I had set up for them — as much as I was projecting my issues onto them — the less I was seeing what they might really be able to teach me. Just the week before I'd asked Kate #2 what she did when her husband was away. "What do you mean, what do I do?" she said. "I feed the cat, I watch television, I put less sauce in the saucepan." The lesson there seemed to be something I wasn't letting myself do. Something about getting on with it already.

"Anyway," Josh said. "I don't see how

this documentary is really your story to tell. How is at all related to what you really wanted to do? You know, finding an uplifting outcome. A happy ending. Isn't that your thing?"

"I don't have a *thing*," I said, even though that wasn't entirely true. One of the reasons I'd gotten interested in the idea of making documentaries in the first place was because I was intrigued by the idea of the "Hollywood ending," people always associating the term with meaning a happy ending, when in reality it seemed to me that the truly classic Hollywood films — like *Casablanca*, *The Graduate*, *Chinatown* — often had endings that were, at the very least, more uncertain than happy. More mixed than any one way. I had always been interested in the idea of trying to make documentary films, chasing around real-life stories, that would have the happy ending I couldn't seem to find anywhere else. I wasn't about to admit that now.

"Besides," he said, "I'm not only talking about this *project*. I'm talking about how you used to be funny. Funny and real and tough."

"I'm tougher now than I was."

"Not even a little," he said.

We were all the way in the right lane. If Josh didn't get over right now, he was going to miss the fork for the interstate. We'd have to turn around at the next exit and circle back. We'd lose a half hour or twenty minutes, at least.

I started to tell him, but he interrupted me. "It's like you're waiting for Matt or something," he said. "It's like you're just staying there because you're waiting for him to come back and get you."

I felt something tighten in my throat, hard and round, numbing me from the inside out, making it very hard to swallow. Making it hard to do much of anything. I didn't know how to explain it to Josh without sounding crazy that I did, for a while, have this recurring fantasy of opening the front door and seeing Matt standing there, his hands down deep in his pockets, looking back at me. Us picking up — not where we left off, but a little before that. When things were still good between us.

Did it matter that Josh used to like Matt? I felt like reminding him of that, but I knew Josh didn't want a catalog of days Matt had spent with our family: the basketball league they had been in together, the time we all ran a half-marathon, the

Chicago trip Matt came on to celebrate my mom's birthday. Josh only cared that Matt wasn't a part of our family now — only cared about my accepting that, once and for all.

"I don't get it, Emmy," Josh said. "You're the one that left him, remember? Even if you didn't get too far afterward."

I wanted to fight back and ask him exactly how far *he* had gotten since things had ended with Elizabeth. It couldn't be that far if, the day before his wedding, he was still going to see her now.

I felt like I was about to cry. Josh was right. I wasn't tough, not anymore. You said a few words to me — a few things that hit wrong — and I was a wimpy ball of emotions. Someone tapped on me, and there I'd go, bouncing.

Josh looked my way, and even though I was averting my eyes, he must have realized he had gone too far because I saw his shoulders slump, and he quickly changed his tone.

"Look," he said. "I'm not trying to be a jerk here. I just don't like you being at this standstill. You could do a hundred different things. Go back to film school, or move to London for a while. You used to love London, remember? Why don't you try to get a job there? Or move somewhere else, and actually get a real job. I'm just saying . . . there's not only one way to go."

I made myself swallow, clearing my throat. "Well, I'm glad to hear that, Josh," I said. "Because you just missed the exit."

A little after nine, we pulled off into a truck stop for breakfast and coffee. We were only about fifteen minutes south of Narragansett, less than sixty miles from Pascoag. But I wanted to stop then, as opposed to any closer to where I lived. Or exactly where I lived. It would be too much to take Josh to the one dinerlike place in Narragansett, Dad's Breakfast Shop, which was a small single-room restaurant just down the street from my house: bright flower paintings, long countertop, regulars who came in every morning and ordered the exact same thing — a #1 (two pancakes, three eggs, and juice), or #2 (corned beef hash and onions, large coffee), or #3 (banana waffles and whipped cream, applesauce on the side).

I could just picture Josh staring at Dad's front door — simultaneously hoping and not hoping that someone would walk through it that I would say hi to, someone that would signal I had something of a situation there resembling a life. Either way, it was inevitable that both of us would have been disappointed.

But this anonymous truck stop was packed with people I wasn't supposed to know. We sat in the corner booth, and Josh ordered a platter of eggs and turkey bacon. I said I wasn't really hungry, but then I ate half of his and got my own order of mini-pancakes and raspberries. I had eaten the night before right before the fireworks. And then at the fireworks, I had eaten that hot dog. And, still, it all felt like a very long time ago.

Right after my food showed up, the cell phone rang. MOM came up flashing on the caller ID screen. I held up the phone so that Josh could see it for himself. We were in trouble. I knew it. I knew *she knew* that something was going on.

"Pick it up," he said.

"You pick it up," I said, trying to hand him the phone.

"No way." He pushed the phone back toward me. "Don't be paranoid. Pick up the phone and find out what she wants. She probably just wants to tell you something about the caterer being late, or last-minute guests canceling. Or how messy you left your room."

It was ring four. He didn't say anything else, but he kept looking at me, waiting for me to do what he said. I gave him a dirty look, but then I picked up the phone anyway.

Our mom was midway through a sentence before I even said hello. She was whispering. ". . . The Moynihan-Richardses are broiling chicken. On the caterer's grill in the backyard. I'm watching through the kitchen window."

I tried to picture her huddled into the corner, leaning up against the window frame — incognito in her green sweat suit — the curtain pulled back just enough so she could get a solid peek.

"You're lying," I said.

"Would I lie about something like that? And can you tell me, please, where did they even get the chicken? Not from me."

I didn't know what to say to her.

"Who eats chicken? For breakfast?"

I put my hand over the receiver. "You need to talk to her," I mouthed to Josh. *"Please."*

He shook his head, and pointed toward the stick-figure sign marking the men's restroom. Then he got up and headed that way.

I took my hand off the receiver.

"Not to mention the fact that your father's a mess," she was saying. "What did you give him to drink last night? He had a beer for breakfast and is saying crazy things about hairs of dogs."

Dogs. Crap. I didn't want any further reminder of where Josh and I were headed. We'd be there in an hour now, less than an hour, and who knew what was waiting for us after that? Who knew what was waiting for him?

"You two should just stay away from here this afternoon, okay? Stay away until five or so, if you can. The fewer people here, the better."

I let a deep breath out, glad for some good news. At least we weren't going to be suspicious for staying away from the house all day, wouldn't be missed. We'd just be following the rules.

"Now, what's going on with you?" she said. "How is everything? How is Meryl holding up?"

"Oh, well, you know Meryl," I said. "She tries not to let these things really get to her."

"You know, that's funny," she said. "Because that's exactly what Meryl said when she called here a few minutes ago looking for you guys."

I felt my eyes opening wide in disbelief. Total panic. She knew we weren't with Meryl. She knew! I looked in the direction of the bathroom, but Josh had disappeared inside. I considered hanging up the phone, pretending later that we'd just gotten disconnected. She would keep calling back, though. I knew this. I knew she would leave a good seventeen messages on my voice mail if she couldn't get through.

"I can't believe you lied to me," she said.

It didn't seem like the ideal time to point out that it was Josh's note, Josh's lie. But I wanted to. I wanted off the hook. Twenty-six years old, and — inside — I was still a tattletale.

"But you know what? It doesn't matter," she said. "You don't need to tell me. Because I already know. What do you think? He's my son. Obviously I would know something like this. And don't give me any of your niceties about how Josh doesn't want to worry me. Since the twenty-one and a half hours I was in labor with him, I've lived the majority of my life worried."

I moved my now-empty plate farther away from me, the smell of leftover syrup starting to make me queasy. "Easy with the imagery," I said.

"The point is," she said, "if Josh didn't want to worry me, he wouldn't be off easy-riding."

"Easy-riding?"

"You know, getting on a Harley. Cruisin' down the highway."

I looked at the receiver as if it would explain to me what the hell was going on here. "Who is this?" I said.

"All I'm saying, Emmy, is that I saw Josh's face when we were watching that movie the other night. The *Erin Brockovich* movie with Julia Roberts. Josh was looking at that motorcycle rider who played her boyfriend. Talking all about Harley engines, and how taking care of one of them properly was like taking care of a patient. Like I was supposed to be excited that he could talk intelligently about such things. I knew what he was thinking. When can I get myself on one of those? And let me tell you, I wasn't impressed."

Josh sat down at the table and gave me a look of disbelief that I was still on the phone.

I put my fingers to my lips for him to stay quiet.

"Just one question. You're not planning

on going also, are you? You know what that's called? Enabling. What you need to do is try to stop him. Because he thinks this is his last window of opportunity. God knows Meryl won't let him go. But he'll listen to you. He'll listen to you before he'll listen to me."

Josh was staring at me. "What's going on?" he mouthed. "What is she saying to you?"

"I hear you, Mom," I said, looking at Josh.

"Good. Because if you tell him not to do this," she said, "he won't."

We passed the Pascoag town line right around 11:00 a.m., the sign for Hamilton Breeders not long after that. The sun was shooting down strong, and we had all the windows open, the air conditioner on us. Josh took a left onto the long dirt road right beyond the Hamilton announcement — a little blue arrow, directing us to there. Everything around us seemed to be getting woodsier: thick trees and long, broken branches, logs covering the thin road. But eventually we came upon a second blue arrow directing us left and then a third one pointing us right, and before I knew it, we were pulling into this large clearing and underneath a tall archway into wide open space. The sky hit down on acres of land, little hills, the forest now just a canopy in the distance.

To the left was a large fenced-in field, several low-riding chain-linked dog pens, matching white dog runs. To the right was a large white farmhouse, and — behind it — a misty lake. As we pulled in, the dogs all ran out, in succession, barking loudly. It was the first time I'd ever seen a bullmastiff, let alone several. They kind of looked like small horses. Protecting their empire.

I turned and looked at Josh. "This is where she lives?" I said.

"This is where she lives," he said. And he was nodding his head, proud, like he was responsible, like it was his home too.

I'd anticipated him getting more nervous now that we were actually here. But for the first time that whole weekend, Josh had a smile on his face. A real smile. He was just sitting there nodding and smiling. And he looked totally relaxed.

"Hey," I said. "You know what? Why don't I make myself scarce for a while? I'll go back into the town, get a cup of coffee or something. There was that happy-looking place Mr. Doughboys. I'll go back there and get myself a doughnut and wait a bit."

"There's no reason to do that," he said. But he wasn't even looking at me anymore. He was already unlocking the car door, getting out. I wasn't sure he knew what I was saying.

Then I heard yelling, and I looked up to see a young woman emerging from the house, telling the dogs to calm down. She was wearing baggy jeans and a white tank top, her hair pulled back in a long blond braid. Even from a distance, I knew she couldn't be a day over twenty. She was heading toward our car, and then, when Josh stepped outside and she saw who it was, she started to run. Josh started running too, and when he reached her, he picked her up in his arms, hugged her to him.

I wasn't sure what to do, so I got out of the car too and walked toward them. Up close, I could see that my estimate had been wrong — Elizabeth wasn't even close to twenty. She was more like fifteen or sixteen, *maybe* seventeen. Soft blue eyes. Young skin. Immediately I had this feeling that this couldn't be happening. I wasn't really here in Rhode Island with these huge dogs and beautiful, baby-style Elizabeth and Josh — who was apparently a very dirty old man. I stopped a few feet away from them, crossing my arms across my chest, standing on the sides of my feet awkwardly.

But then he introduced us.

"Emmy," he said, "I'd like you to meet

Grace Hamilton. Also known as Princess Grace."

Princess Grace started laughing, and held out her hand to me. "It's very nice to meet you," she said.

I shook her hand back, and attempted to say something like nice to meet you too — though my throat was kind of closed up, and it came out wrong, came out only about half-finished, much closer to just, "meet you."

Josh kept smiling at her, thoroughly enjoying, apparently, seeing her laugh. "Grace is Elizabeth's daughter," he said.

Elizabeth's daughter. Her *daughter*. I felt myself take a breath, unaware that until then, I hadn't. This wasn't Elizabeth. I felt so much relief — so deep-seated and complete — that this wasn't turning out the way it looked at first that it took me a minute to focus on the implications of what I'd just found out. Elizabeth had a daughter. I was shaking this girl's hand. All of which meant, that at the very least, this complicated situation had just gotten even more complicated.

I didn't have too long to wrap my head around it, though. Because right then, the front door swung open and out walked Grace's older version — same jeans, same

142

braid — heading straight toward us.

Elizabeth. She was darker than her daughter was — with sharper eyes, olive skin. She definitely wasn't as classically pretty as Grace. She wasn't as pretty as Meryl either, for that matter, but there was something about the way she was carrying herself — this assuredness — that you couldn't help but notice. It was almost like she was about to teach you something.

This might be part of the reason why when she first saw Josh, unlike Grace, she didn't start running toward him. Instead, she stopped moving. So did Josh. The only one moving then was Grace, who was looking back and forth between Josh and Elizabeth, almost frantically.

She kept her hand on Josh's arm, but I think if she had been thinking about it, she would have let him go. She was obviously looking to her mom for clues as to what she was supposed to do. So was Josh, who — even in the intensity of this bizarre standoff — was still smiling ear-to-ear, like a total and complete dumb-ass.

"Hello there," she said.

"Hello there," he said back.

Then she looked toward me, and her face softened a little — the lines around her mouth letting loose. And I could see it — what I had almost missed before I could see what her smile did to her — how pretty she really was.

I wasn't sure what to do, but I felt the need to do so something. So I uncrossed my arms and gave her a small hip-side wave.

She gave me one back. "Hi, Emmy," she said.

"Yes, thank you," I said, which made about as much sense as it sounded like it made.

Then she motioned to Josh, and for a second — just a split second — I could tell how happy she was to see him there in front of her. Almost as happy as he was to be there.

"You should move the car out back behind the house," she said. "We have someone coming to look at the new litter in a little while." She was already walking away.

"When is a little while?" Josh said.

She turned back around to face him. "You in a rush to get somewhere else?"

He shook his head. "No."

"You sure?"

I wanted to hide, anywhere, waiting for him to answer.

"Positive."

She looked at him like she didn't believe him, but she nodded all the same. And then, when she started walking away from him again, heading in the direction of the dog paddocks, Josh turned around himself and did exactly what she said.

The only other time I'd been at a dog breeder was with Matt, the summer before his senior year of college, when we were down in Delaware at his old roommate's mother's house. While the guys helped her with a project in the attic, the roommate's mother set me up with a pitcher of iced tea on her back porch, and staring out the window, I noticed that the backyard next door was full of slides, and dog pens, and animal runs leading out to an open field. I walked over to the fence separating the yards to try and learn more. It turned out the couple next door were dog breeders, breeding very expensive terriers — the tiniest of dogs, almost doll-like — that, even as adults, were able to fit into the palm of a hand.

On first glance, these bullmastiffs seemed like the exact opposite. The adult dogs were the biggest dogs I'd ever seen —

well over 100 pounds, closer to 150 — oversize bulldogs, angry and big-cheeked. Open-eyed. And, at first glance, they looked a little scary. They looked more than a little scary. Up close, they looked more sweet-faced than anything else, and I started to remember having read somewhere that, if properly socialized, bullmastiffs were arguably sweeter than terriers — arguably the sweetest breed of dogs in the entire world. They wanted to be your best friends and to protect you and be dedicated to you and — if you asked anyone who had ever owned one of these dogs — to make your life feel more complete.

When we walked into the farmhouse, Grace handed me a pamphlet that explained all this. The pamphlet was blue and gold, with slim, gray writing. It looked so familiar that I couldn't help but wonder if I had seen it somewhere before — like Josh's Boston apartment — and had just discarded it, forgotten to ask him why he had it in the first place. Why would I assume it was important? That it hadn't just been left under his windshield wiper somewhere? I had no reason to assume it would lead me here somehow. Now that I was here, though, I read it carefully. I was done assuming anything for the time being. The

147

pamphlet explained that hobby breeders, like Elizabeth, didn't make a living raising these dogs — it was almost impossible to — even though the dogs cost upward of $1,500. If you were lucky and doing the job well, you stayed out of the red. This was what you hoped for. This was what you hoped for so you could keep caring for the dogs — raising them and showing them and placing them in homes they'd really like.

On the back of the pamphlet was a photograph of Elizabeth and a small bio that said she was a holistic veterinarian. What the pamphlet didn't say was that, for Elizabeth, breeding was a life she'd fallen into right when she met Grace's father at nineteen. And now, even all these years since he'd left their life behind, she happily stayed. Every Monday through Wednesday, she drove down to her veterinary practice in Providence and saw her patients. And her patients' parents. The rest of the time, she was here. I didn't find out that part until later. All I did know for sure walking around the farmhouse was that it seemed like a different world here. And I knew part of it was coming from me, coming from how I often idealized things that weren't familiar. Still, it was like I was seeing everything through the lens of a smoke screen: the landscape coming through the windows candied and iridescent — the farm both taking on this magical quality, and being more definite than any place I could remember visiting.

I followed Grace into the kitchen, which looked like the inside of a boat cabin. There was a lot of dark wood and photographs, an old record player. Flowered candles were everywhere. It was all very pretty, but it also smelled a little funny — like something was burning.

"Sorry about the smell," she said, as if she could hear my thoughts. "I was working on a science project last night. I had to make glue from scratch."

"How did that go?"

"Fantastic," she said. "If glue doesn't have to stick."

I smiled at her, probably bigger than I meant it. Josh and Elizabeth had gone for a walk somewhere, and I had no idea when they were coming back. Which left Grace and me to fend for ourselves, at least for now. But I wasn't entirely unhappy with this arrangement. I couldn't imagine that they were having a very pleasant conversation, and I figured having us around for it wouldn't help too much. One look at Elizabeth before, and I knew that she knew what Josh was supposed to be doing this weekend. I guess the question was whether she also knew he was going to show up here first, and what, if anything, that might change.

Grace opened the refrigerator door and started taking out supplies — vegetables and meats, a thick loaf of bread. "I thought we could make some lunch, maybe," she said. "How do turkey clubs sound?"

I could still feel the bacon in my stomach. If we didn't cook, though, what were we going to do? Sit here and talk about Elizabeth and Josh? Me just grilling her on all the details that didn't matter as much as the main two: Josh was supposed to get married tomorrow; he was still here now.

"Turkey clubs sound great," I said.

"Great," she said, and smiled at me. Then she handed me a package of bacon, and a large yellow pepper. "So did you guys drive all the way here from New York this morning? I mean, did you do it all in one day?"

I unwrapped the bacon cover, started separating the strips. I was about to answer her that it had taken us just under four hours — not really so bad — when she started talking again.

"Because the time Josh and I did it, we hit traffic right around New Haven. Some sort of ten-rig truck accident. And it ended up taking us forever. We ended up missing the play that we were going to New York for in the first place. We ended up driving all the way there for a cheeseburger."

I stopped moving, the bacon in my hand now midair. "Just the two of you?" I said before I could stop myself.

Damn. I felt bad as soon as the words were out. But hearing about the two of them planning something like a trip to New York City was like an enormous reminder — as if I needed another one — of how deep this situation with Elizabeth really ran. How involved it all was. He had taken her daughter to New York. He had come back here to take her home. To take them home. Upstairs, in the master bathroom, there was probably cream that only he used. There was probably an extra holder for his toothbrush.

Grace closed the refrigerator door and reached into the cabinet for cutting boards, two oversize knives. "It was a really good cheeseburger," she said, almost apologetically.

I immediately tried to change my expression so she wouldn't feel judged by me. The only person I was judging wasn't even in this room, and it wasn't even that I was judging him, exactly. Or maybe I was, a little. And maybe that wasn't helping anything either.

"Look," she said, all the equipment still in her hand. "Maybe we should make a rule that we don't talk about either of them. Or else I'm going to say something else you don't want to hear, and you'll keep looking at me in a way that makes me realize you don't know much of anything about me. That whatever Josh has told you, it hasn't really been about me. And that will just make me feel bad."

I nodded in agreement. I didn't want a sixteen-year-old trying to make me feel better. And I certainly didn't want her doing a better job of making sense of this situation than I was able to do.

"I think that's a good idea," I said.

Grace smiled. Then she handed me one of everything — cutting board, knife. I leaned up against the counter and began cutting — and tried to do exactly what she'd asked for. Each strip was the same size, sandwich-ready.

It seemed really important to have something to focus hard on because I knew when I looked outside the window, I'd see something I didn't want to see: Josh and Elizabeth out in the distance, up on the hill. I couldn't help it. I looked anyway. And there they were out in the distance: sitting cross-legged across from each other. Close, but not touching.

Josh was leaning forward, listening intently to whatever Elizabeth was saying. The weirdest part, though, didn't have anything to do with Elizabeth at all. It had to do with Josh. He looked older sitting there — or maybe older is not the best way to explain it. He looked like he was trying harder. There was just something missing in his face — that cocky look, that absence-ness, that, even if I couldn't always name it, made me think he'd never fully grow up.

Meryl liked to joke that being with Josh was less like dating a doctor and more like having a child. She would do the laundry, most of the cleaning, most of the taking care of. But she never seemed to mind it — the opposite was true, if anything. Elizabeth, on the other hand, already had a real child to care for. And just watching Josh and Elizabeth now — watching how he was the one leaning in to her, how he was the one concentrating — I had an inkling that despite the messiness of this situation, Josh didn't have that same dynamic with Elizabeth. That, here, he wanted to be the one to do the caretaking. And I couldn't help but wonder if that was part of the reason that he was in his current situation — he both longed to be the type of partner Elizabeth would need, and feared he couldn't be.

I turned toward Grace, who had started frying up the bacon. "How are you doing over there?" I asked.

"Good," she said.

"Good," I said.

When I'd left Matt, Josh was the one who went into the city and got the rest of my things: my clothes, my photo albums, my favorite books and movies. He was the one who brought everything to me in Rhode Island, helped me begin to settle in there. And he didn't ask me any questions. Not then. He didn't make any judgments. He just stayed with me until I told him it was okay for him to go. One way or the other, who was I to judge him now?

"Hey," Grace said, "Could you grab me the peanut butter out of the fridge?" she said. "I need to grease the pan a little."

"You can use peanut butter? In a frying pan?" I said.

"Well, we're out of oil, and we're not

doing the weekly market run until to-morrow. So I'm thinking it's either that or the non-sticky glue," she said, shrugging.

"My choice?" I said.

She nodded. "That's what I'm trying to say."

After we finished preparing, Grace and I sat across from each other at the kitchen table. We had matching monster sandwiches on our plates, oversize scoops of sweet potato fries. Through large bites, Grace explained to me that even though she was only sixteen, she had already finished high school — Elizabeth had let her skip first and eighth grade — and was University of Rhode Island bound in the fall. She was going to study marine biology there. She was accepted into the honors program to do it. She was given a scholarship to do whatever she wanted.

"I'm just commuting for now, though," she said. "I'm not sold yet on the whole college and academics thing."

"Yeah, I can tell you must be pretty lousy at it." I smiled at her.

She shrugged. "No, I guess I want to go. I just feel like I'm a better learner outside of school, you know? I know that sounds stupid, but I think I'll learn more around here or heading to the ocean. But my mom says I need the degree, and I know she's right."

I picked up my sandwich, nodding, but also trying not to be too vehement about it. I didn't want to undermine what Elizabeth had instilled in her, but I did totally understand what she was saying. I was someone who was pretty lousy at school. I did what I could to get by. But my goal was never really to learn anything that they wanted me to learn. In fact, as soon as I was supposed to learn something, I spent all my time trying to figure out something else. The immigration paper I was supposed to write in high school turned into my quest to understand elevator construction. My freshman-year foray into Pavlovian psychology turned into a quest to learn about ballroom dancing in China. I could only look into things well when someone wanted me looking at something else.

This reminded me of what I was supposed to be learning now, what lessons I was hoping to be taking from the wives. I was so stuck on wanting to see one particular thing from them, I was a little worried I was missing it, what I was really supposed to be learning.

I turned and looked at Grace. "You

know, if commuting gets tough or something, you're welcome to stay at my place. I
live right near URI," I said. "Like fifteen
minutes away, tops."

"Yeah?" she said, nodding at me in a way
that told me she already knew that. Josh
must have told her. I fiddled with my sandwich, trying not to think about what else
he must have told her. Trying — even
harder — not to worry about how he was
doing right now. What was or wasn't being
decided.

Grace put her sandwich down too,
blushing a little. "I'm a little nervous about
meeting friends, and stuff. Maybe you can
show me what people do around there for
fun."

"Oh, I would, but I don't have any."

"Fun?"

"People."

She smiled, and then stood up and
started cleaning the table. "You know," she
said, "your brother used to joke with me
that if we never talked about school, we
wouldn't have to go back. To just ignore it
when anyone said I needed to do something to get ready."

I had been standing up to help her, but I
stopped, mid-stand, just froze there. And I
must have started looking at her funny,

which may have scared her, but probably because she thought she'd broken our deal to not discuss them. She hadn't broken the deal, though — or at least it didn't matter to me anymore. How could I explain to her that, in ways I wasn't entirely ready for, different things were starting to?

I tried to recover, quickly, saying the absolute first thing that came to my mind. "So I noticed the lake," I said, pointing in its imagined direction. "It looks a little like wrapping paper from a distance. You know, that shiny kind. I'm always wrapping it wrong, putting the shine on the inside. Does it look like that close up?"

"Maybe a little," she said, and started to laugh, which let me know it didn't. "But we could go sit by it, if you'd like. Pick up a couple of the dogs and bring them with."

"Not the big dogs," I said, before I could stop myself. "You know what? Let's just go."

The pamphlet Grace had handed me in the house explained that in every litter of bullmastiffs, there was the alpha dog — usually the firstborn, always the main protector — that the other baby pups tried to stay near, cuddle into, and ultimately emulate. Then there was the runt. The runt was essentially the alpha dog's opposite: smaller, weaker, the scaredy-cat of all its brothers and sisters. Ironically, it was the one that was often considered the most aggressive dog because it was more prone to bite. It was prone to try to prove how tough it was.

It didn't matter that I read this on the way to the paddocks. When we got there, I was drawn to the littlest dog in the litter anyway. Hannibal. Apparently, his name hadn't predisposed him to prowess. Grace, on the other hand, let out Sam, the biggest dog. The alpha. Hannibal had all of Sam's features: same chocolate skin, same heavy jowls — all of it just much smaller.

This might be why — despite all evidence to the contrary — I thought it was a good idea to reach straight into his pen and pick Hannibal up myself. Before Grace could stop me, or reach over and control the situation, my new pal Hanny rewarded me by digging in — teeth first — to take a nice-size chunk of skin off my wrist.

"Oh, my gosh," I said, dropping him to the ground. "He bit me."

Grace raced over to survey the damage. I turned my wrist over to show her. Right by my wrist bone — where skin used to be —

I expected to see a small, red moon. But there was really just a tiny scratch.

"That doesn't look too bad," Grace said, reaching into a pocket and coming out with a Band-Aid. "It could have been a lot worse." She looked down at Hannibal and gave him a scowl. "Not nice!" she said to him.

"Can he hear you?" I asked, blowing on the non-wound.

She picked Hannibal back up, patting him on the head. "She just needs a lot of touching," she said. "She has to learn that that's safe."

I looked up from putting the Band-Aid on my wrist. "He's a she?"

Grace nodded, reaching into her pocket and taking out an oatmeal cookie.

I shook my head as she tried to hand it to me. "I think I'm okay for now," I said.

"No," she said. "Give it to Hannibal. If you feed it to her, she'll trust you more."

The thought of putting my hand near her mouth again wasn't too appealing right then. But I put the cookie up to her lips anyway, like Grace showed me, letting her lick it off my hand, rubbing her head with my free one.

"We just have to be extra careful with the runt generally, and spend more time," she said. "Not less. Less gets you into trouble."

I pulled my hand away. "Sounds like most people I know," I said.

We headed down toward the lake, Hannibal in Grace's arms, Sam in tow behind me. Grace seemed happier — or more comfortable, at least — now that the dogs were around. When we got down to the lake, she sat herself down on the edge and took her shoes off, put her feet right in the water. I followed suit. It didn't feel so nauseatingly hot when our feet were in the water. I felt, automatically, a lot cooler — and happier — a chill racing up my spine for the first time all day.

"You want to know a secret?" Grace said. "Well, maybe it's not really a secret, but you want to know the real reason I don't want to leave here?"

"There's a boy," I said for her. "He's the reason?"

"How did you do that?"

"I'm not that old."

"You're pretty old," she said.

"I am," I said. I put my head in my hands, shaking my head. "How did that happen?"

Grace started laughing. I looked at her and smiled. I hadn't been that much older than her when Matt and I started dating. And I remembered it so clearly — that feeling at the beginning — that incredible feeling that this was the first real thing that had ever happened to me. I wanted to tell anyone who would listen: my mother, my friends, the mailman. Even if I couldn't articulate it at the time, I think I believed that talking about Matt made us more real, somehow, more permanent. In some way, maybe it did.

"The thing is, he's a year behind me in school," she said. "He has a year left here, but the problem is he doesn't want to go to college at all, even when he can. Except maybe the community college here, which is pretty terrible."

It was called Baruch. Baraque. Something like that. I had seen it driving in. The entire campus was composed of three small buildings, a circular driveway. No ocean access that I could see.

"He wants to just stay here and keep everything like it is. His family has these two flower shops. One here, one the next town over. And he'll be fine. He can do that forever, and be content. He wants to do that forever."

"What do you want?" I said.

"I want to keep him happy," she said.

162

I looked down at the water. Sam was standing right on the edge, getting closer to waddling in. Hannibal was busy digging, nestling into my side headfirst. I reached out, gingerly, to pet her. My junior year of college, Matt had been a finalist for a great internship at an architecture firm in Chicago, and he would have taken it, wouldn't have let us being apart from each other stop him at all, if they had taken him. It was the first time I questioned my own decision to attend NYU instead of going out to California like I'd originally planned. It wasn't that I didn't want him to go, but it had been such an easy decision for me to choose being near him, keeping him happy. I couldn't understand why, all those years later, our being apart wasn't a harder one for him to make. It took a long time for me to understand that the fact that I feared him going contributed to him not being scared himself. That was often the truth. Someone's affection would give someone else freedom.

"I just think if I stay here for the year and commute, we'll figure it out, you know? He'll see college isn't so weird. Maybe he'll want to come with me the next year." Grace shook her head, almost angrily. "I just think people forget what it feels like to really be in love, you know? Like when that's the only thing in the world that matters. I just don't want to decide it's not that important. Do you know what I mean by that?"

I knew exactly what she meant, which made it harder to figure out how to tell her what I wanted to say, which was that it wasn't always everything. Love. And still, what did I know? The reason Matt and I hadn't worked out wasn't because I loved him like that. It was because he stopped loving me like that. And really, why did that have to be the end of the story? I had made it the end because I was too scared about what might be coming next — some watered-down version of what we'd once been. What had come next instead? Me, motionless, unable to do much without him. The watered-down version of what I'd once been.

"So did you have a serious boyfriend when you were in high school?" Grace asked. She put her hands in the lake to wet them, petting Sam's back, cooling him down.

"Kind of."

She looked at me, confused. "Kind of serious?"

"Kind of high school," I said. "He was

164

already in college when we met. It's a long story."

"How did it end?" she said, but before I could even answer, her brow was tightening, her eyes getting nervous. And I could tell she wasn't wondering about Matt and me anymore, not really. She was wondering how she could avoid it happening to her.

"Do you miss him?" she whispered.

Every day, I wanted to say. "You know, I wouldn't compare it really, anyway," I said. "I think it sounds totally different. For starters, I just wanted to keep him happy."

She licked her lips, forming the beginning of a laugh. "Man. I really walked into that one, didn't I?" she said.

"Look," I said. "The truth is that no one can know. That's what no one wants to tell you. It may work out beautifully between the two of you. You may celebrate your seventieth anniversary, right here, by this lake. Despite whatever you do or you don't do. It's happened before," I said.

"It has," she said. "It has happened . . . I wish you could meet him. You know what? The shop's like fifteen minutes from here. We could go stop by. Or I could call him, and he could come by here. I know he'd love to meet you. I know he'd love to meet Josh's sister . . ."

Josh. Where was he now? How was it that in the midst of all of this, I had managed to forget about him, forget about what was at stake for him, if only for a couple of minutes? Maybe because part of being here let me realize it. How much was at stake, even besides him. I looked down at my watch. Almost two. If we left right now, we would be home with enough time to get ready for tonight. If that was what he wanted. But only if we left right now.

"Oh, sorry. Forget it," she said. "It's probably not the best time for introductions."

"No, I'm sorry. I'd like to meet him. It's just that I don't know what Josh is doing."

"Who does?" she said. Then she shrugged, wiping her wet hands on her jeans. "Besides, what can meeting someone really tell you anyway? What did you tell from meeting my mom? I know you didn't really get to, but can I tell you something, then, honestly? I mean if I told you Josh and my mom were like that, like that much in love, would it make you want to throw up?" she said. "Would it be so corny that you'd have to puke?"

I smiled. "I'm not going to puke."

"You sure?"

"Pretty sure."

"Because they'd always just do this thing, you know, after they thought I was sleeping," she said. "They'd come down here and dance by the lake. They didn't even bring music. No CD player, no radio. They'd just dance. And I know everything else. I know he's had a girlfriend for a long time. I know it's hard for him to imagine leaving her. I know he wasn't honest about it with my mom. I get all that. But what about the dancing? Especially because they'd always do it so well together. I mean, *really* well. Like they were hearing the same song or something."

I looked out at the lake. The world I knew felt so far away. Everything but this felt far away and imaginary and untrue. And I knew the rest of it would come screaming back soon enough. But for a minute, just one more, I tried to hold it. So I'd remember. So, whatever happened, I wouldn't decide that this wasn't true too.

"I just don't understand how the same thing can be playing in both of their heads like that," she said. "If it isn't love between them, how did the same thing get there?"

A few minutes after we made it back to the kitchen, Josh and Elizabeth got back from their walk. Elizabeth came through the door first, Josh right behind her. His shirt was off — the long-sleeved one that had been under the short-sleeved one — now he was just wearing the short-sleeved one. And they weren't talking to each other. I tried to read the situation, but I wasn't sure how. It didn't really seem like a bad kind of not talking. It didn't seem like they were about to leave each other again.

"Hey, guys," Josh said, patting my back as he walked past me at the table and over to where Grace was. "How's your day been going?"

He tried to give me a smile. I tried to give him one back, but I think my attempt was even less successful than his.

"Emmy got attacked by Hannibal," Grace said, as Josh bent down beneath her chair.

"You all right?" Josh asked, turning toward me, but it was Elizabeth who came over quickly, looking for where.

I put out my wrist to show her. "I'm really fine. There's barely even a scratch," I said. Trying to point it out to her, I actually had trouble finding it.

Elizabeth turned toward Grace. "That's not funny to joke about, Grace," she said.

Grace gave her mother a look and turned back toward Josh. "It's a little bit funny," she said to him. "Don't you think?"

"Absolutely," he said.

Then he wrapped his hands around the back of her chair's legs and moved in closer. At first I thought I was having déjà vu or something — the scene looked so familiar. It took me a second to realize that this was how my dad used to talk to us when he was trying to explain something. Like the time I burned my hand on the grill and didn't tell him all day because I thought I'd get in trouble for touching the grill when I knew I wasn't supposed to. It was this way he had of looking right at us from a certain angle so that we knew he still loved us — whatever he was going to say to us next. Josh was talking low, and I couldn't hear what he was saying, but

Grace was nodding her head, softly, in agreement.

And it did something to me — warmed my heart a little. Because I could see it for a second, even if I felt conflicted about admitting it. It wasn't about which woman Josh ultimately chose — it was about which *Josh* Josh chose. If it were a version closer to this one, that would make all the difference.

I wasn't sure what to do now. Elizabeth, who had been watching them also for a minute, had left the room. And, so, I followed her out into the living room, where she was sitting on the couch. I sat down next to her, tentatively at first, right on the couch's edge. There had been none of the *this is Elizabeth, this is Emmy* stuff — not really — and now didn't seem like the time. It didn't seem like a time to make small talk for that matter either, and I was fairly certain Elizabeth would have been happy to sit there in silence, but I wasn't evolved enough for that yet.

"So, I think your daughter's great," I said. "She's your daughter. So I'm sure you know that. Well obviously you know she's your daughter, but you probably also know she's great . . ."

"She likes you too," she said. "I can tell."

"You think so? That's nice to hear." And it was. It was just weird how that could happen — how you could know someone for so little time, but feel like you've gotten to know that person in the most important ways. A version of Josh's five-minutes theory, I imagined. Kind of how you could know someone forever and never really know him or her at all: time not getting to be the only measure anymore of how well you paid attention.

I looked down at my legs, tried smoothing out my wrinkling dress over them.

Then Elizabeth looked over at me. "So, Josh says you are working on a film? About fishermen's wives, right?"

"That's right."

"He says you're having a little trouble finishing."

I made myself look at her. "You could say that."

"Grace and I switched fortune cookies at dinner the other night, because hers said, 'You can't finish the things you weren't supposed to start.' She was so freaked out that we kept trying to think about all the examples of that not being true. Different relationships or jobs or even movies we'd only sat through half of. A hundred things.

But even though I don't usually take advice from fortune cookies, I have to say, the more we were trying to prove the argument false, the more I started to think there might be some truth to it."

I didn't say anything. But inside, I was thinking: This is a reason to dislike her. Isn't that what I wanted? I had just met her, and who'd asked her to philosophize about my life? Only, looking at her, I couldn't deny that she didn't seem to be trying to preach to me. She seemed to genuinely want to help me figure something out. Something about where to go from here.

"How far along are you?" she asked.

I tilted my head from side to side. "Not far enough that I feel like I'm really getting anywhere," I said. "But too far along to stop."

She smiled again, the same affectionate smile she had given me outside before, as though she could tell this was the first hard thing I'd said to her. The first thing that was solid. It made the truth seem kinder.

"So the film's not the reason then?" she said. "That you're staying in Narragansett?"

I started messing with my dress again,

thinking about how to answer that. I could tell her that maybe I was staying in Narragansett because it was so nice there. That would be something she could understand, wanting to live somewhere beautiful. Only, that didn't sound anything like the truth. "I don't really know," I said.

She looked at me and didn't say anything, but it made me stop fiddling, made me feel comfortable, like I didn't need to be nervous with her. Like she already knew me. And I couldn't help but think that maybe she already loved me a little because she loved Josh so much. And maybe I already needed to love her for the same reason.

"I know it's not my place," she said. "But be nice to your brother this weekend. You might feel mad at him about all this, but be mad next week. Or the next week after that too, even. This weekend, just try and take care of him a little. He'll need it from you."

"Okay." I said. Then I said something that surprised myself. "Is that when you're going to be mad at him?"

"I don't think you get to be mad at someone unless they come through for you. I don't think you have that luxury. I think you think you can be mad, but really you're just doing something else."

"What's that?"

"Waiting."

I looked at her, hoping she would give away what she was feeling, but she didn't seem to be giving too much of anything away. I did see this look in her eyes though, a confident look, like she knew how all of this was going to turn out, like she'd always known, and it was just a matter of time until Josh caught up. I couldn't help but wonder if that was what love was — believing that someone was going to come through, in the end, and that it would still count.

Josh walked back in, and we both stood up as if he had caught us in the middle of something. Grace snuck past Josh in the kitchen doorway and went to stand by her mother. I figured that this was my clue to go and stand next to Josh, but I didn't much feel like it. I wanted to stay where I was. I wanted to have dinner here. I wanted to go swimming in the lake. Okay, well, maybe I didn't want to go swimming in the lake, but it was looking a whole lot better than my alternative. But Josh gave me a look like it was time to get going, and so I nodded my head in agreement, because really, what other choice did I have?

"I'll talk to you later," he said, turning to Elizabeth, who didn't really make a move toward him from where we were standing.

"All right," she said. If I was right, though, and I thought I was, she said it in a way as though she didn't believe him. Or maybe it wasn't that she didn't believe him, but more that talking later wasn't the point. The point had already passed, today, with him *not* doing something, and they both knew it. This was just what you did afterward.

I started to follow Josh outside, but then I turned back around. I turned back around to face them. "I can't believe how great it is here," I said. "I really love it. Maybe more than I've ever loved any place in my whole life."

Of course I didn't say this out loud — only in my head. Out loud, I still couldn't seem to say a thing.

Elizabeth did it for me.

"It was good to meet you, Emmy," she said.

"It was good to meet you," I said.

Then I turned and looked at Grace. I wanted to run over and hug her, tell her again that she was more than welcome to take the drive forty miles south, and I'd show her around URI. That I'd get some people if it would make her come quicker. I wanted to tell her that even though I'd just met her, I so much wanted to know how things were going to turn out for her — with her boyfriend, with school, with everything. I wanted to know it, even at the very moment it was happening.

But when she looked up and met my eyes, she gave me the hang-loose sign — thumb out, pinky up — and this seemed more right.

So I hang-loosed her back, like it was something I knew how to do, and let that be my good-bye.

In the car, Josh wouldn't talk.

He gave me the keys and got in the passenger side, reclining the seat all the way back. I took a right back onto the dirt road and then the two lefts off of the property, heading toward the highway. Everything was still a little smoky, and hidden in the heat. I didn't look in the rearview mirror or over toward Josh, even once. Meanwhile, the blinker — my broken blinker — was acting up again and nonstop blinking again and making me crazy.

"You want to turn that off?" he said, irritated.

"I am trying here," I said, gripping the

steering wheel more than a little too tight, making nothing happen.

The interstate was creeping up on our right. I was going to turn onto it. For better or worse, I was going to move us farther and farther away from this place. I was going to have to go home and promise our mother that I hadn't let him do anything bad. I was going to have to take a shower. I kept waiting for Josh to stop me, to say something. But he didn't. Once I merged on — once all that was ahead of us was interstate — I ended up being the one to break the silence.

"Did you have sex with her today?" I said.

"What?" He shook his head, disgusted. "What does that even have to do with anything, Emmy?"

"Well, I want to know, Josh," I said. But the truth was, I didn't want to know if that happened. Not really. It was just the only thing I could think of that was concrete, certain, that might give me a clue as to what he was going to do.

He kept his eyes window-side. "No."

"No, you didn't? Or no, you're not going to answer me?"

"Emmy, I need a minute here, okay? I need like sixty seconds to pull myself together."

I wanted to tell him he had 180 miles worth of seconds to do that, but then he'd be put in a position to answer much harsher critics than me. And, more importantly, if he didn't talk to me now, he might not talk at all. He might just let this go, too, because there wouldn't be enough time in his mind to do anything else.

"Look," I said, "when this is all said and done, I'll have driven eight hours with you today, and met two really interesting people, who obviously mean a great deal to you. Who seem to make you a different you, if that makes any sense. And now I have to go back to Scarsdale and deal with all of this, too, so I'd like it if you'd let me know where your head is at. Whenever you're ready."

"You don't want to hear me right now," he said. "You just want to be mad at whatever I say. And maybe you should be. Maybe it was wrong to ask you to come today. But can you please just focus on getting us home in time for tonight's dinner?"

I started to ask him if he was still planning on going to tonight's dinner — as if that cemented anything either way. But before I did, before we could get into it, one way or another, I saw police sirens flashing behind us. I looked back down at my dashboard. I was barely five miles over the speed limit. I was barely even three.

"That can't be for us," I said.

Only it was becoming more apparent that it was absolutely for us. The state trooper was on our tail, still flashing, the sirens making their noise now, waiting for us to respond.

"Oh, you've got to be kidding me with this," Josh said, looking in the rearview mirror.

Then he turned and shot me a dirty look.

"What?" I said, pulling over onto the divider. "This isn't my fault."

"Am I the one driving?" he said. "Am I?"

I shook my head, slowly rolling down my window. On the other side was one of the oldest police officers in the history of any police force, ever. He had a curled white mustache and was wearing a hearing aid and a police officer's cap — not to mention a pair of old-school Ray-Ban sunglasses on a cord around his neck. He was a few ten-minute steps shy of a walker.

"I'm Officer Z," he said, pointing at the nametag on his jacket that said OFFICER Z in block-brown letters. "I'm going to need all your information, miss."

Josh leaned across me, handing my registration over. "Can you tell us why we were stopped, Officer?"

I gave him my license. I could see Z reading over it carefully, and I knew he was doing the math in his head. Was I even old enough to drive? Out here on the highway?

"Excuse me," Z said, picking up his walkie-talkie, which had gone from full-fledged static to mumbled talking.

I took the opportunity of the distraction to turn toward Josh and say something to him. But he stopped me with his hand. "Just," he said. "Don't."

Z put his walkie-talkie away and returned his attention to us. "Do you realize," he said, handing the license back to me, "that your blinker is still blinking? And has been for the last several miles?"

"I know, officer," I said. "I'm sorry. My brother and I will get it fixed as soon as we get home."

"Where's home, dear?" Z said.

"New York."

Josh closed his eyes and slowly began shaking his head.

"There will be no driving to New York in this automobile," he said. "That would be a considerable hazard."

I turned toward Josh, who I was sure by this point was having visions of us wandering down the highway, calling Berringer and waiting the three hours and change for him to come and get us.

Which was when it occurred to me that this would only ever happen today — this nonsense with Officer Z, being pulled over for this blinker crap — that the universe only delivered up moments like this in the *one* moment when what you needed was the exact opposite.

"Oh, I'm sorry, officer," I said. "Did I say New York? I meant the next exit. Home is the next exit. See, I'm in graduate school near here at the University of Rhode Island. I'm not driving to New York right now. No, sir. I just meant that we're not going to get the blinker good and properly fixed until we get home. But we're staying in Rhode Island tonight. We're staying in Rhode Island for the whole week, in fact. I promise. We're off at the next exit."

Z looked skeptical, but slowly he handed me back my papers. "I'm going to have to escort you to there, I'm afraid. Just to make sure that no one's feeling inclined to take any chances."

"That would be good, Officer," I said. "More than good. Great."

Z started to walk away, but then — just

as I was about to tell Josh that we'd get back on the Interstate on an exit three exits away from here, less than twenty minutes away — Officer Z turned back around.

"Don't let me catch you on the interstate further down the line," he said. "I have friends all along the way. Believe you me, you'll be sorry if that happens."

Then he offered a final nod and began the inevitably disheartening walk back to his automobile. Josh was taking maps out of the glove compartment.

"Now what?" I said.

"Now," he said, picking one of the maps out of the bunch on the floor, "I hope you know some back roads."

"Back roads? Josh, we'll never make it home in time that way. We barely were going to make it in time taking 95."

He didn't even answer me, shaking his head fiercely, eyes scouring the map.

I pulled back onto the highway, Officer Z right in front of me. "Excuse me," I said. "But how is it my fault? I'm not the one who needed to make this trip today. None of this has anything to do with me."

He flipped the map over to the other side. It was completely upside down now. "Emmy, I'm trying to concentrate here," he said. "I have to figure out what I'm doing."

No kidding, I wanted to say. But I refrained.

He tossed the map back onto the ground. "You know what?" he said. "When you get off the highway, let me drive, okay? I'll feel better that way. You'll navigate or something."

I said that would be fine, but as far as I knew there was nothing *to* navigate. The only way back to New York besides the interstate required going through Narragansett, something I wasn't particularly eager to do right then. And, still, I made the first necessary left that would wind us the long way down Boston Neck Road, leading us to Route 1. Then I pulled the car over and swung into the passenger seat. Josh walked to the driver's side and we were moving again.

On the left, soon enough, we'd be passing the beach, the ocean and Little Clam restaurant, Narragansett's tiny pier. I looked out the window the other way. Because somewhere out there in the distance, right before Little Clam — right after the pier — was where I lived. In someone else's house with someone else's things. A light not on, a window not even open, nobody at all at home.

"Isn't there someone you could call?" Josh said. "Someone whose car we could maybe borrow for the weekend?"

I thought of everyone who I knew well enough to call: my boss Bobby, who as part of his renewed marriage arrangement wasn't allowed surprise visitors at home, the carless Martins from next door, the 107 wives, none of whom I wanted to bother with this. With all of my questions for them, they were always trying to figure out information on me beyond the brief bio I'd provide for them. I didn't want to start by introducing them to my brother and explaining what we were doing here the day before his wedding.

The only person who seemed like a real possibility was this guy Cooper, who was less my friend and more a guy who just came into the shop a lot now that his girlfriend had left him. I was pretty sure that he didn't like me, but I think he kept hoping that if he met me again, he might.

"I know this one guy," I said. "He lives right behind the high school. We could stop by his place, if you want."

In truth, we had to stop by Cooper's because I didn't have his phone number to call. Of course, I didn't offer this part up. I just directed Josh left and then right — waiting for Narragansett High School to appear before us: the low-rise brick building, empty summer parking lot, the Arthur L. Stewart Football Field. Cooper's house was right past it — the football field — a small, broken-down colonial.

Only, when we got there, we had a little problem. In front of what had been Cooper's house, there was a large For Sale sign with a red Sold sticker running diagonally across it. There was a turned-over empty garbage pail in the driveway. And stacked-up, unopened newspapers. Cooper's car was absent.

"Tell me this isn't where your friend Cooper lives," Josh said. His hands tightened around the wheel, his knuckles losing their color. I knew he was afraid to turn toward me. I knew he was afraid of what else he might say.

"Obviously," I said. "Not anymore."

Josh pulled quickly out of the driveway, heading west. He was too angry to even ask me which way he was supposed to be going now. He was too angry at me to ask anything.

I turned and looked out the window and didn't say anything again, not until we were passing by the tackle shop — the small-hominess of it — which, for inexplicable reasons, lifted my spirits. It occurred to me that I could take Josh inside and show him around. Everyone who came in there would know who I was. And if we stayed long enough, one of the wives would probably come to visit me. But there was no way Josh was pulling over now — not for anything — least of all for my attempt to convince him this wasn't a bad way for me to live. Both of us, I think, were too worried about the way he was living.

I turned and looked at him, carefully, afraid before the words were out about what I was going to ask him.

"What did you say to her, Josh? What did you say to Grace when you and Elizabeth got back from your walk? In the kitchen. You looked so serious. What did you say to her then?"

He kept his eyes on the road. "I told her I'd be back soon," he said. "I told her I'd be seeing her soon."

"Will you?" I said.

He didn't say anything at first.

"Josh?"

"I really hope so," he said.

He looked so upset that I turned away from him and looked down at the floor.

Which was when I saw it. The shiny pink invitation. For June's daughter's birthday party. Holly's birthday party. Was it really just yesterday that I'd passed June in the tackle-shop parking lot, staring into her crowded wagon? That I had made the silent wish that I'd end up seeing her again today?

Now the invite was staring up at me, like a new promise, the beginning of a different idea.

"You know what, Josh?" I said. "Take a left up there at the light. Take a left and a right and pull in to the first yellow house. And then get your things together."

"What are you talking about?"

"I may have a way," I said, "to get us home."

It was 7:30 on the dot when we pulled onto Drake Road in June's red Volvo station wagon, thirty seconds after that when we pulled into our parents' driveway. We couldn't actually get deep enough into the driveway — the wagon part of the wagon was still sticking into the street — because there were already so many automobiles crowded in there: two Volkswagen buggies with "Lydia's Florists" written on the side, an oversized silver van, a two-story catering truck. The valet guy was already in place, wearing a white tuxedo jacket. A couple in a gray Cadillac was making their way slowly toward him.

"Are you kidding me with this?" Josh said, attempting to back us out.

He was struggling, as he had been the whole way home, to see over all the junk in the backseat, the very large Papa Smurf doll covering up most of the back window. I had tried to move it when we hit the Connecticut border, but I only made it worse.

"What are we going to do now?" he asked.

I started to answer him, but stopped myself when I realized it was more a rhetorical question. Josh was already making his way down the block and around the corner to the Wademans, whose backyard ran straight into ours. In our younger days, Josh had showed me this shortcut into and out of our property, for emergency use only: early-morning sneak-ins, late-night sneak-outs. You just shimmied past their old oak tree — tire swing intact, even though the children had been gone for over a decade — past Mrs. Mason's tomato garden, through the first row of bushes, and then the second row, which separated their home from ours.

This was the first time we'd ever done it together. When we made it through the last set, we were standing at the top of our backyard, looking down over the hill at the rest of it.

Tonight, it was full of people milling around, trays already clattering, and right at the center, a rectangular white tent, which, from where I stood, appeared all airy and light — almost like a cloud against the night sky.

Everything was all set up inside the tent: white tea rose centerpieces, thin white tablecloths, floating candles glowing everywhere. The waitstaff was standing by all the tables pouring water into glasses, rearranging everything that was already perfectly arranged.

I bent lower so I could see this.

Josh bent lower too. "I see the Wademans in there already," I said. "Do you see them? At the corner table, talking to Dad?"

There they were, huddled over in the corner, Mrs. Wademan, looking a little like a floating candle herself in her large hooped dress. Dad was standing right beside her, bending forward toward where Mr. Wademan was seated.

"What do you think they're talking about?" I said.

"What do I think they're talking about? Who cares what they're talking about? Who gets to a rehearsal dinner early? Really. I want to know."

He was losing it a little.

"At least we know they're not going to bust us for blocking their driveway," I said.

"I didn't block their driveway."

"You didn't *not* block it."

Josh turned to me. "Do you have any suggestions? For what we're going to do now?"

I bit on my lip, surveying the situation again. The majority of the backyard was clearly off-limits to us. I knew we were going to have to make a run for it, if we wanted to make it inside undetected. It was tricky, though. There was a little more wiggle room to the left of the tent, but the door there led right to the living room/ kitchen area, where we were more likely to run into people. The other option though — right of the tent, toward the farther door — led right past our dad. The real question was whether our mom was near him. Because right now she needed to be avoided at all costs.

"Maybe we should separate, and race inside," I said. "That way, if Mom catches one of us, we can say the other is upstairs showering. We can make it like we've been home for a while."

"Emmy, I'm not going to make a run for it. That's a ridiculous suggestion. You think I'm that scared?"

But then, before I could explain my rationale — before I could convince him that a run-in with our mother in his dirty T-shirt wasn't in his best interest right now — he was gone. He had taken the right-side option, and was running down the hill in long strides, covering his head as he passed near our father, moving faster than I could ever remember seeing him move.

This left me to go left. But just as I was down the hill, heading for the clear, I heard Mom calling out my name from a few feet behind me. I stopped in my tracks, unsure what to do next.

"Don't you even think of walking away from me," she said, making the decision for me.

I turned around, giving her a little wave. She was wearing a long silver sheath dress, drop earrings, her hair pulled into a tiny bun. She gave me a less-than-friendly wave back. But as soon as she was up close to me, I hugged her. And as she pulled away, I could tell she wasn't mad anymore. She couldn't even pretend to look mad at me anymore. I had her like that.

"I don't know where you've been," she said. "I don't even think I want to know right now. Dad had to order an extra air machine because it's still so hot out here. A huge air machine to blow air into the tent. Do you have any idea how much something like that costs? Three thousand dollars! What kind of situation is this?"

I touched her face, trying to calm her down. "You look beautiful," I said.

She touched mine back. "You look a little tired." Then she looked down at my wrist. "Oh, my God," she said. "What happened?"

I followed her eyes down to the spot where Hannibal almost got me. "Nothing."

She ran her fingers along the invisible cut. "This is clearly not nothing," she said. "Does this look like nothing to you?"

"Yes, actually."

"What is going on, Emmy? Please tell me. I can't make anything better unless you are willing to talk about it."

And right then, I wanted to so much. Not only because I didn't want to know about Josh's situation alone anymore, but also because she would know how to help him — she would know how to fix this — better than I did. But I couldn't stop thinking that maybe Josh wasn't ready to have this fixed. Maybe, whatever was going on here, it wasn't ready to end. Not quite yet.

"Okay, so if you're just going to stand there in silence, then I at least want you to go rub your wrist with alcohol, and wrap it in a bigger Band-Aid. They're in your bathroom under the sink. Put two on, if you don't mind. Layers are always good. Then get dressed for tonight."

I nodded. "Okay."

She kissed my forehead, my scratched wrist. "Okay."

I started walking away.

"Oh, and Emmy." I turned back around. "FYI, if Mrs. Wademan comes up and asks you later, I told her Steven Spielberg was interested in buying the fishermen's wives film you've been working on."

"What are you talking about?"

She shrugged. "She wanted to know what you were doing in Rhode Island, and so I told her what you were doing."

"Mom, Steven Spielberg's not interested in buying my documentary."

"Well, as far as I'm concerned, he should be."

I looked at her in disbelief. "Are you crazy?"

"Are you two hours late?"

I wasn't sure there was anything to say to that.

"Now, on your way upstairs would you mind stopping in the basement and checking on the Moynihan-Richardses for me? I just need you to make sure they're doing okay down there. People are getting here. Do you understand what I'm saying?" She was leaning in my ear, whispering. "I really don't want any more incidents involving fowl."

"I'm on it, Mom," I said.

"Thank you," she said. "And Em? It wouldn't hurt to put on a little makeup for the photographs," she said. "Just a little right on your cheeks. Even your dad's wearing some."

"He is not."

She nodded. "A little rouge," she said.

"Mom, he isn't."

"Maybe not," she said. "But the point is, he would if I asked him to."

When Josh and I were little, we used to like playing with rings of keys. Every Sunday, in fact, my father would take us to the hardware store right at the Five Corners, and we were each allowed to pick out one key to put on our respective key rings. Then we'd go home and run around with flashlights downstairs in the basement and laundry room, pretending we were on some type of covert operation and our keys could open any door we needed them to unlock.

This memory came to me as I started down the stairs to check on the Moynihan-Richardses, and I could tell that the main light wasn't on down there. The light wasn't on and the air wasn't on, and upon closer inspection, it didn't seem like anyone was even down there. I flipped on the switch just to be sure, but I didn't see the Moynihan-Richardses anywhere. I didn't even see evidence of the Moynihan-Richardses anywhere, except for a small black suitcase, which was standing upright, clothing plunging out on the sides, totally packed.

I imagined them sneaking off into the night, with only their keys, thinking better of subjecting themselves to the scrutiny of all the unspoken questions certain to fly their way later this evening — everyone wanting to understand why two relatively successful professors chose to give up a child for adoption. The way Meryl had explained it, they just didn't believe they would have been good at rearing a child. Something told me they probably weren't entirely wrong on that front.

"Dr. Moynihan-Richards?" I said, calling out into the strange emptiness. "Mrs. Moynihan-Richards?"

I got no reply.

"My mom just wanted you to know that you're welcome upstairs at the party. Whenever you're ready to come upstairs." This was great. I was talking to no one. "Or, whatever you want to do. Your decision," I said.

I headed back up the stairs, closing the door tightly behind me, but not before I turned the light switch off again — brightness disappearing behind me — in case that would make them ready to come out.

In my room, I found Meryl standing in front of the one wall mirror, four wide, round curlers in her hair, putting her makeup on. Her dress was already on: a short, black lacy thing that fell mid-thigh. She looked gorgeous. Josh was sitting on the bed behind her, watching her in the mirror, his hands folded on his lap. She was concentrating really hard on the lip gloss application, and — I thought — she didn't notice me.

I started to creep back out of the room, undetected, but then — when I had one foot still in the doorway — Meryl turned toward me.

"Hey, you," she said, holding her lip gloss midair. "You running away without even saying hi to me? I know I'm not exactly the world's fanciest bride here, but still. Don't I deserve a little attention?"

"Of course," I said, curling my hands behind my back. "Of course you do. I wanted to say hi to you. I just have to go to the bathroom. I have to go the bathroom pretty badly."

I looked over at Josh, who was looking at me so apologetically that I almost forgave him for making me a part of all of this. Then I turned back to Meryl, who looked — even in curlers, even half-ready — so polished, so graceful. She had tried over the years to impart to me all those things that came so naturally to her: had shown me how to wash my hair in horse shampoo, how to let the guy lead when you slow-dance, how to eat oysters on the half-shell. Anything she could do to offer up the things that having a big sister did for you. How had I repaid her today? By being, at the very least, untruthful? At the most, disloyal? Questioning, even now, if this was where Josh belonged? It was too much for me. I started hopping from foot to foot, remembering my lie about having to pee.

"We've been in the car forever," I said. And as soon as the words were out, I could feel my eyes opening wide, worrying that I'd slipped — that Meryl didn't know we'd been driving, but she just opened her arms to signal me in for a hug. I really thought I was going to be sick.

I moved toward her anyway.

"Josh was telling me what happened on the way back here with Officer Z," Meryl said when she pulled away. "Is that really his name? Sounds like you two had a little road-trip adventure today."

I looked over at Josh, confused. Why was he telling her about Officer Z? Certainly not because he had disclosed what we were doing in Officer Z's territory to begin with. I wondered, though, if it made him feel better to tell her things somewhere near the truth. If that made the lying seem smaller. I tried to piece together in my mind where he'd told her we were. Maybe Rhode Island, still, but for me — not him. Maybe Josh had said he had there with me today because something troubling was going on with me.

"I'm just sorry, Meryl," I said. "That

we're so late. We didn't want to be. We didn't mean to be."

"My God," she said. "Don't apologize. I was just hoping you would have gotten back earlier, so we could have watched some of your tapes together. I want to see a little of all this research we keep hearing about. I bet you're getting somewhere amazing with all this."

I looked into the corner of my room where I had left them — the tapes — but the garbage bag wasn't there anymore. I felt a panic start to rise. But before I could go anywhere with it, Meryl followed my eyes to the same corner spot.

"Oh, I moved them. I'm sorry. I should have told you right away that I moved them. People have just been coming in and out of here, and I didn't want anything to happen to them. I put them in the corner of your bathroom to keep them safe. I figured there would be less ground traffic in there."

Then she looked back at Josh, her smile all gone, her eyes looking all worried. And I wondered, again, what it was she knew.

But Josh just shook his head. "Don't do it," Josh said.

"Don't do what?" I asked.

He kept shaking his head, his eyes still down. But Meryl was facing me again.

"Look, I know Josh wanted me to wait to tell you," she said. "But I can't. I can't look at you and wait. I can't stand you not knowing when I know you'd really want to know. Oh, I'm making it worse. I should just say it already, shouldn't I? I know I should."

I looked back and forth between them. The way this was going down, I had no idea what was going on. It wasn't possible — was it? — that he had told Meryl about Elizabeth already. It couldn't be. I was no more than five minutes behind him coming up here. You couldn't fit an explanation into that time even if you wanted to try to fit one in. There would be more questions than answers. There would be a need for significantly more time.

And then Meryl took a deep breath and started to talk.

"I ran into Matt today," she said.

I knew I must have heard wrong. I was so sure of it that I just kept looking at her, not saying anything.

She nodded her head. "A few hours ago," she said.

"My Matt?"

"Your Matt."

I had no idea what to say. I couldn't even begin, really, to get a handle on what that might have meant. I just kept envisioning scenes in my head: the two of them walking down that same stretch of Fifth Avenue near Union Square, or hitting the same street corner near Grand Central Terminal, Matt leaving the architecture firm — where he'd started putting in Saturday hours — to have a cigarette, Meryl on her way out here. Or maybe they had been near our old West Village apartment. Still Matt's West Village apartment. Two-eighty-five West Street. A small, dilapidated townhouse in between two gentrified townhouses. Owned by one person each. One family each sharing the space we shared with nine other apartments.

I felt it so strongly, the smell of that hallway: its inevitable blend of cherry alcohol and dried fish. We'd stayed up all night the night we moved in, hopelessly lighting scented candles to cancel out the smell, Matt painting a miniature solar system on our bedroom ceiling — Orion's belt in one far corner, Vega the strongest star in a summer sky in the other. An Olympic sprint runner eventually moved upstairs. He would do a thousand jumping jacks, nightly, right above our heads. Above those stars. It became a little like living in an earthquake.

"Come sit down for a minute," Josh said

now, moving down on the bed farther, making room for three of me.

Meryl motioned to the bed too. "Go sit," she said.

And I could see from the way they were both looking at me, I must have been doing something scary. By the way Meryl was reaching for me, I must have been walking backward. I was walking backward without even realizing it — right out the door.

"Just sit down on the bed for one minute, babe," Meryl said. "I'll explain everything."

But before she could even start, I realized how much I didn't want to hear. If she saw him today — if she saw Matt — he was okay. He was walking somewhere, where he would have to be okay to walk. Whatever else she wanted to tell me about the run-in — if she wanted to tell me he was in love with someone or moving to Alaska or that he hated me — I couldn't hear it.

"You know what? Just give me a second, first. Okay? Before you tell me anything else, I really have to go to the bathroom first. I already told you guys that. I really have to go."

And then, as fast as I've ever moved in my life, I raced toward the bathroom, mine and Josh's, and shut the door tightly behind me. Is there any way to explain this moment without it seeming dramatic? I was seeing stars. I was seeing great white blocks in front of my eyes. I was seeing nothing.

I shut the door tightly, curling my knees to my chest, my back tight against the frame. I reached up to lock it. Then I saw it, gently squeezed into the far corner. My bag of tapes. The bright blue drawstring tied, like a heart, on the top, keeping it all in: everything I had or, more accurately, hadn't managed to accomplish in three years away. What had Matt been doing over these three years? Were there things in his life — designs or relationships or some combination of both — that he couldn't manage to finish either? That he couldn't even really start?

I turned around and reached under the sink — deep back into the cabinet, hidden beneath an old rag — for my small cigarette stash, four years old now. Almost five. I didn't care. I knew they were still there. I knew they were still there precisely for a moment like this.

I found the pack and the matches and lit one up and took a really long drag and almost threw it up. But I smoked it. I smoked it, and felt better and felt worse and got ready to light another one.

Before I did, though, I said a small, silent prayer of gratitude that tonight was going to end. Not gracefully, maybe, but eventually. Because I wasn't coming out of this bathroom, for anything, until I really believed that this was true.

part three

The only rehearsal dinner I had gone to in Rhode Island was for Diane #1's only son, Brian, who was — at the time — on his fourth wedding, and not yet thirty. I suspected I had procured the invitation because there were only so many people in town who weren't friends with one of the first three brides.

I didn't care why I was invited, though. I was glad to be there. They had made it a drum-party rehearsal dinner because Diane had read somewhere that rehearsal dinners used to be very noisy affairs — that this was a luck thing. That, in fact, parties were originally held on the eve of the wedding day in order to chase away all the evil spirits that wanted to descend upon a couple and effectively jinx any hope they had of starting a good life together. The idea was for the rehearsal dinner to be very loud and rowdy: the more noise, the better. Evil spirits, apparently, were scared off by that type of chaos. Diane's husband, Brian senior, spent most of the night banging on the makeshift Caribbean drum for dear life. "We're not taking any chances," Diane said, shaking her head. "We can't afford to do another, if this one goes south."

Unfortunately for Josh and Meryl, if noise at the rehearsal dinner was a true indicator of future happiness, they were off to a questionable start at best. There were no drums, makeshift or otherwise, no noisemakers, not much noise to speak of, in fact, at all.

This was what they did have: a lone flutist playing quietly in the corner, white helium balloons covering the top of the tent, and huge bowls everywhere full of floating ivory lilies.

Everyone was walking around in their soft dresses and blue neckties, patting each other on the back, drawing kisses in the air. Eventually, we all found our way to our respective tables, and dinner was served, family-style. All of it was just like Meryl had asked for. We passed around large platters of barbecue chicken, spicy cashews, shrimp, and mixed salad. There were heaping silver teacups full of dark scotch and Russian vodka. And, in the middle of each table, circling the tea roses, were chocolate-covered strawberries.

After dinner, my mother walked to the front of the tent and announced that there were wet-naps in a bowl on each table. She held up hers as demonstration: more stewardess than hostess.

She pointed out the make-your-own chocolate chip cookie sundae bar catty-cornered in the back, as if anyone could miss it. You have never seen so many sweets: licorice and gummy bears and candy raspberries and brownie bites and peppermint chews and soft fudge. Baskets of jellybeans, and frosted cinnamon sticks. Six different kinds of ice cream.

"Help yourselves," she said.

I took my wet-nap out of the bowl first. It was wrapped in a small blue Tiffany bow.

"You've got to be kidding me," I said, but I tied the bow around my wrist anyway. Meryl's mom Bess, who was sitting across from me, winked at me when she saw me do it.

Then she did the same thing.

It had been just the two of us for most of dinner — her husband having made friends with the bartender, my parents and

Meryl playing hosts, Josh on the other side of the tent offering constant help to the help, staying as far away as possible from anyone who might actually want to talk to him. And the Moynihan-Richardses' seats had never even been sat in.

"It's like you and I are starting a trend here," she said, pointing proudly to her wrist.

"Kind of," I said.

There was talk that the M-R's were around here, somewhere, hiding out at a corner table, and other talk that Mrs. Moynihan-Richards hadn't been feeling well and so they were back in the basement now. No one seemed to know for sure, and Bess — at least — didn't seem to care too much.

"So, are you getting excited for to-morrow?" Bess said.

This wasn't the first time she had asked me this question. We were starting to struggle with each other. It wasn't making any of it easier that I had long ago lost sight of any joy in tonight, my mind peri-odically shifting through different images from today, over and over, as if part of a broken-down slide show. In one, Elizabeth was sitting on the couch, in the other Meryl standing in my bedroom. It didn't seem possible that they existed in the same world. They weren't supposed to, which I was sure made it that much easier for Josh to separate them, to let each count in her own space. The fact that I could understand, now, how that could be done was making me feel worst of all.

"Tomorrow's supposed to be a scorcher, you know," Bess said. "Even hotter than today. Meryl's father heard a hundred and four! I'm lucky I moved the ceremony inside, is all I have to say. Who wants to be in heat like that?"

"No one," I said.

"No one," she repeated, fiddling with her bow. "So what part of tomorrow are you looking forward to the most?"

That was it. I stood up. "Bess," I said. "Would you excuse me for just a second? I'm going to help myself to a sundae. Can I get you one?"

"Sugar is the devil, dear," she said. "But enjoy yourself."

I started to walk toward the sundae bar, a specific plan for the rest of the evening in sight. First, I was going to get two scoops of vanilla and a scoop of chocolate and two homemade cookies. I was going to find a corner to sit in, and eat the whole sundae as slowly as was humanly possible. Then, as soon as a departure wouldn't be worthy of any attention, I was going to go inside, take off this uncomfortable dress, and go to sleep.

Only my well-thought-out plan had a way of falling apart mid-stride when I saw him standing there — right by the sundae bar — older, yes, but looking pretty much the same: same curly red hair, soft chin, still a good two inches shorter than me. Justin Silverman. Recent Northwestern Law School graduate. Junior high boyfriend. Future husband.

I didn't know what to do. The thought of small talk now — the thought of any talk at all — was just too much to handle. Especially with him. Especially with my mother, out there in the distance, pretending not to watch us, and being so terrible at the pretending. I turned back around, way too quickly, and ran headfirst into Berringer's chest.

"Easy," he said, catching me by the elbow, trying to steady me. "Running away from someone?"

I looked up at him, the strange angle of his chin. He was wearing a blue tie and dark sports jacket, jeans.

In his right hand, he was holding a large plastic cup.

"You look so nice," I said.

He smiled. "You look so nice."

I followed his eyes down to my own dress: a long red halter, tied tight in the back, right at the top of my neck. My mom had picked it out while I'd been gone. Even on sale, which I knew it was, it had undoubtedly cost more than I had made at the tackle shop all last month.

Berringer held the cup out in my direction. "Cookie Crisps?"

I peeked inside, and there they were: a cupful of them brimming up to the top, a plastic spoon stuffed into the cup also.

"Dude, if my mom sees you eating those, she's going to have a nervous breakdown."

"Did you just call me dude?" he said.

"Maybe."

"Well, rest assured, I have a whole game plan to make her think they're part of the sundae bar. If it even comes to that."

I watched him take a too-large bite, catching some milk with the back of his hand.

"It's going to be fine," he said.

From the sundae bar, I could feel eyes on me, bearing down right into the back of my head, the top of my shoulders. Before I thought better of it — before I remembered why I needed not to — I met them.

Justin Silverman, balancing against the sundae bar's pointy corner. He smiled in my direction, giving me a nod. I gave him one back before turning back toward Berringer.

I knew it. I was trapped. I couldn't very well go back to the table. Bess was still sitting there, Meryl standing over her, her camera around her neck. She unhooked the camera and took the seat next to her mom. And I couldn't really make a beeline for the house either — the patio full of people, my mom blocking the main back door.

"You know, Josh is looking for you," Berringer said. "He's out front unloading a van."

Josh. A whole other story. I kept my eyes down. I didn't want to be with Berringer anymore either. I didn't want to start telling him about the day, about Elizabeth and Grace and the farm. I didn't want to *not* tell him. But before I could excuse myself graciously, a girl from across the way waved. She was tall and dark-skinned and gorgeous — the kind of girl who could tie a silk scarf around her neck and not have it be ironic. She could wear polo pants or capris or a long thick braid. Tonight she was wearing a short beige dress, toeless stiletto heels. She matched the party. And she was coming right our way.

"Is that your girlfriend?" I said.

"Celia?" he said, waving back at her with his free hand. "Yeah, that is most definitely Celia."

I felt a little sick. I maybe even felt more than a little sick, which could have been why I was only picking up pieces of what Berringer was saying next — something about how he didn't even know if Celia was his girlfriend, per se: she did live three thousand miles away from him, after all. When she was even in the country. She'd been in Manchester for the last four months. She was going back there next week. It was relaxed between them, really. It was a relaxed situation.

"I want you to talk to her, though," he said. "She's really into film, and I was talking about you earlier. And she was actually saying that an old buddy of hers is an independent film producer, and he might be able to help you out with your documentary. When the time comes. You know, with distribution or putting you in touch with the right people at least."

I nodded as if to say, Great, even though it was anything but. Even though the only help he could give me at this point was to help me figure out a way to finish it. And I didn't want it from him anyway. And I really didn't want it from her.

I started backing up, trying to be casual about it, straightening out my dress while I went, straightening out the bow on my wrist. "You know what? I'm actually trying to get Bess a sundae," I said. "I need to get Bess a caramel sundae, I promised her. And she wants a big one. And there are things. There are other things . . ."

He pointed toward the sundae bar, which was in the other direction. "You're heading the wrong way, then," he said.

I followed his finger with my eyes, just in time to see Justin making his way toward me. "Well, would you do it then, Berringer? Make her one? She's over there." I pointed at the table, where I'd just left. "Lots of extra caramel sauce. And get one for Meryl too, okay?"

He took hold of my arm. "Give me a sec, first. Josh is looking for you."

I didn't know what to say to that. I didn't really want to see Josh right then, let alone listen to him talk more about how he didn't know what to do. I wanted to know what he was going to do, which apparently was the one thing he wasn't able to tell me.

But when I didn't say anything,

Berringer gave me a dirty look. "Emmy," he said. "What are you doing? You need to try to be supportive." He started whispering. "There's other things on the line here besides your opinion of the situation."

"Oh, there are other things on the line? Wow. How could I forget that?" I gave him the dirtiest look I could conjure up. Berringer and his horse-riding girlfriend. Cereal-eating bastard. "Well, last time I checked, in fact, I was being pretty damn over-the-top supportive. But you know what? If you think you can do a better job, Berringer, then the next time he wants to go to Rhode Island to meet his other girlfriend and her teenage daughter on the day before his wedding, have him give you a call. Bring Celia along. She can ride shotgun."

And with that, I prepared to storm off. But instead I backed myself up right into Justin.

"Emmy," he said.

I just stared at him. He was wearing a red silk tie, white lines running diagonally through it. It looked like a life preserver. I didn't even give him a chance to say hello. "Did you drive your car over here by any chance?" I asked. "Is it out on the street?"

He nodded. "It's on the street," he said.

"So let's get going then," I said.

I took his hand and led the way, not turning to see behind me what I knew I'd see: Berringer looking after me, annoyed and confused, the same way I would be looking at him if I'd had the courage to stay there and finish what he'd started.

"You okay?" Justin said, as we made it to the front, him a few paces behind, struggling to keep up.

"Why wouldn't I be okay?" I said.

He gave me a weird look instead of answering. But he was done pushing it. He was done doing anything, apparently, but getting me to his car — getting me there as fast as possible — because I was starting to show it in my eyes. That I was going with or without him.

Meanwhile, on the other side of the party, Josh had finished carrying back yet another case of wine from the bartender's van to the bar. From over by the table, where she was still sitting with Bess, Meryl took a photograph of him placing the case down. Like many good photographers, she was already starting to see, in the dark, what she had captured with her wide lens. She couldn't quite make out that desperate look on his face, but she knew something was there, something off, that was bound

to become more clear — more certain —
when she developed it. It was, after all, becoming a little impossible to miss.

I didn't really want to be in the car with Justin Silverman, obviously, but those of us in need of rescuing can't always be particular as to who our rescuer will be. And what I was starting to understand, driving away from my house, was how very much I was in need of it.

I was trying to avoid looking at Justin, who was confused and a little giddy, talking too fast about midwestern winters and first-year exams and a story about how he owned a bar for a little while or worked at a bar for a little while and had thought about taking it over. He was talking a lot about the Illinois border to Wisconsin. I wasn't blaming Justin, though. It was my fault, if it was anyone's, that we were in his car now, that he was feeling the need to entertain me, to keep this strange momentum going.

This wasn't because he liked me, I was sure. It had more to do with him banking on what we of wedding age had all become witnesses to — how during these wedding weekends, single women, feeling a little lonely, maybe, or just feeling a little too far from being the bride, found themselves loosening their own rules, opting to be more *flexible,* more quickly. Considering my own blundered bridal history and the desperate frenzy with which I'd greeted him, Justin probably thought he was going to get lucky sometime in the next thirty seconds.

"I should tell you," I said as he made a left into Scarsdale Village, "that I really haven't been feeling very well. I think I could be contagious."

He turned toward me, like he was about to say something really important, something like he didn't care anyway, that it didn't bother him. He wanted to kiss me. I knew it. I knew it, I knew it, I knew it. It was going to be awkward and weird. And what was I going to do then?

"I'm sure you can't catch anything from sitting over there," I continued. "I mean maybe you can, but I just wanted to tell you. I just wanted to be honest with you."

He got quiet for the first time since we had been alone together — neither of us saying anything else until the main stretch of town came into view. It was mostly closed down: the Häagen-Dazs ice cream shop and DeCicco supermarket, the only two stores still lit up.

"Emmy, you know I'm gay, right?"

"What? You're *gay?*"

He nodded. "I prefer the term Gay-American."

I shook my head, confused. I wanted to tell him to slow down, but I guess there was no slowing down now. I guess there was no time to do anything, now, but hurry along. Josh's wedding was coming, and the Berringer-Celia nuptials were probably soon to follow, and Matt was in New York City somewhere, and Meryl was waiting eagerly to tell me what she knew about him, and I was in a car with a friend I hadn't seen since right around the time we learned to drive in the first place. And, of the two of us, he was the only one brave enough to be honest so far.

"I was trying to figure out how to tell you," he said. "Not that I had to tell you, but I don't know . . . it was making me nervous that you didn't know. Not that that's the only thing there is to know, but that's why I was talking so much. Do you do that too?"

"Talk a lot when I'm nervous? Yes, and I

also tend to make up illnesses."

"It's just weird coming back here because no one knows. It's strange how that works, you know? We can live a totally different life away from here, and come back and pretend that it doesn't count. Pretend that we're still the same person we were when we left here."

I nodded, because if there were anything I understood, it was that. It was pretending. Justin seemed to understand who he used to be, who he was now. And while I could kind of see who I used to be too. I couldn't say with much certainty who I currently was. Someone's ex-fiancé, a non-committal filmmaker? It was all still too defined by what I no longer had. Did Justin want to hear that?

I turned and looked at him. "So I'm taking it your mom doesn't know, huh? Because I think my mom was under the impression that the two of them were hooking us up."

"Yeah, well, my mother and I tend to have a don't-ask, don't-tell policy," he said.

I shook my head. "I've got to get myself one of those."

He circled around the supermarket parking lot, pulling into a spot right near the ice cream shop.

"The problem is, now there's a guy in Chicago. A great guy. Who is about to be a great guy in New York. At least that's looking like the plan. But not until I tell them. He doesn't want to come until I tell everyone what's what."

"You better get on that, Skippy."

"Right. Tell them. *Tell them.* I knew I was forgetting to do something."

I laughed, thinking about my to-do list: finish my documentary (was that even possible?), make it through this weekend unscathed, help Josh fix his life.

He turned off the ignition. "So now that you don't think I'm trying to jump your bones. Banana split? Unless you have to get back sometime in the next five minutes."

"I definitely don't have to get back any time in the next five minutes," I said, smiling at him.

He smiled back. Then he opened the car door, starting to laugh. "Gay-American. I'm pretty funny sometimes, you know?"

"Wait." I reached for his arm, stopping him. "I think I've got a better idea."

He closed the door, turned the ignition back on. "Excellent. Just tell me where to go."

"That way," I said, pointing in the only direction I wanted.

Of the 24,000 some-odd 7-Eleven stores in the United States, the top ten are named in order each year on a list compiled at headquarters and, then, apparently, made public. And every year, hovering right around number five, is the 7-Eleven located on the corner of Popham and Garth just outside of Scarsdale Village. Part of the reason for this particular Sevies success was that Scarsdale High students long ago adopted this place as their local hangout. Any weekend night — and most weeknights — you'd find the parking lot full of cars you'd recognize: other students picking up cigarettes or listening to music in their cars, sitting on their hoods. I missed so much of that, in the end, missed so much of my high school ending, because I was with Matt.

We tended to go to our own place — this all-night diner over on Central Avenue, where they'd let us order cheap white wine, the very cheapest, the kind that came in the small bottles they'd serve on airplanes. We just preferred it that way, being alone together, than spending time with my friends. We even made a habit of coming back there once I'd moved to the city, once we moved in together. We'd still split six-packs of little airplane bottles, and a large Belgian waffle, and half a container of syrup. We'd just sit there, talking all night about nothing, our legs touching under the table, lightly, the whole time. A whole time ago.

"I can't believe we're here," Justin said, as he passed the bright 7-Eleven sign, parking the car by the old pay phone, under the old rock wall. "It's too weird, you know? It's a little too weird."

I stared out the window, taking it all in. It was great to be back here. I had it all planned out. We'd get a couple of Slurpees and a pack of Parliament Lights and some corn dogs. And then sit in the corner of the parking lot and smoke cigarettes and pretend we were sixteen again.

I felt a smile growing on my face, just thinking about it. The first real smile all day — my house, and everything waiting back there, a little less pressing. But no, that wasn't true. It wasn't the first smile. I had been smiling that morning by the lake with Grace, hadn't I? But was that really just this morning? I wasn't entirely convinced that was even possible.

"You know," Justin said, "I really *hate* to burst your bubble here, as your excitement is very nice. But my little brother says that the kids don't even come here anymore. They go to the Golden Horseshoe instead. They hang out there behind Seven Woks."

"Near the Dumpsters?"

He nodded. "Someone put up a tepee or something."

"I don't want to know that," I said. "Who wants to know that?"

But I started looking around the parking lot. We were, in fact, the only car in there. There could have been a million reasons for that, though. It was a holiday weekend. It was still pretty early.

"What would you do differently now . . . I mean if the gods came down, and made you sixteen again?"

I shook my head, trying to think about it. What were the right answers? Would I not take the chances I took? Would I take different ones?

"Maybe you should give me the magic potion now," I said, "And I'll end up a decade back in time, waking up in my bed all

Freaky Friday like. I'll race to the mirror to check out my face and start screaming."

"Except that you look exactly the same."

"Not exactly," I said.

"Except exactly."

"Anyway . . . I'd get to wish really hard again that I was just right here with you. And that everything was turning out just like it was supposed to."

I said the rest in my head, because it sounded too silly out loud. *And I wouldn't make any mistakes this time, and everyone would still love me, and I'd live happily ever after.* But somehow Justin heard the rest anyway, because he reached for my hand and squeezed it. Then he got out of the car and walked around to my side to let me out too.

"You know, Everett," he said, putting his arm around me. "I'm beginning to think it's a good thing we broke up. It seems a little like you have trouble letting yourself be happy."

I thought of Josh, all the trouble he'd managed to get himself into for the same reason, or something approaching the same reason. I thought of what could be going on back at the house — what probably wasn't: anything zeroing in on honesty, or resolution, or a good-bye.

"It runs in my family, maybe." I said, holding on to his waist. "But at least now, I don't have to feel so badly that you dumped me with no apparent reason in the universe for it."

"No, you should probably still feel bad. That decision had nothing to do with my sexual preference. Really. It wasn't about that at all."

"What did it have to do with?'

"You wouldn't let me kiss you," he said.

I looked up at him, having only the vaguest memory of what he was referring to, an image that I wasn't even sure I wasn't making up right then — of Justin standing before me on the steps, reaching out.

"Don't you remember? Everyone in our homeroom played that game where you had to pay the toll to go inside for attendance? Peter Peterson was the head gatekeeper. And the toll was a kiss, and you made an extremely big deal that you'd rather have gym with Mrs. Gallagher two periods in a row than even do that. Than even kiss me on the cheek."

I didn't know what he was talking about beyond a vague recollection popping into my head of Peter Peterson wearing a Jets jersey. He was standing in the homeroom doorway, his arms crossed, yelling at me about something.

"What ever happened to Peter Peterson?"

"I think he's in jail," Justin said.

"I think that's right," I said. Then I looked at him. "I'm sorry I wouldn't kiss you. I'd be glad to kiss you now."

"Sure, now that you know I don't want to."

"I didn't say I know how to make things easy," I said.

He leaned down, whispered in my ear. "You may want to work on that," he said.

When we got inside Sevies, the first thing I did was head to the Slurpee machine in the back. Meanwhile, Justin ran up and down the aisles, grabbing all the other goodies: two packs of cigarettes and potato chips, a king-size bag of Charleston Chews, four cans of grape soda. I was halfway through filling up the second Big Gulp cup with blue Slurpee mix when Justin got a call on his cell phone.

"Is that Chicago?" I said.

"That's Chicago," he said, dropping all the goodies in a pile on the Slurpee table. "You've got all this?"

"I've more than got it." I smiled at him.

"I'll meet you in the car."

He started to offer me a cursory, Are you sure? But really, he was already halfway out the front door. His phone already up against his ear. I topped off the second large gulp — capping the rim with a dome lid — the whole time my eyes on our prizes, trying to figure out how I'd get them to the checkout counter. I knew I could take two trips, but I didn't want to do that. It felt like a certain kind of failure.

So I maneuvered it like this: a pack of cigarettes under each arm, the sodas and Chews in my left hand, the Slurpees and bag of chips in the other. I looked like a scarecrow or a robot, or a fancy Christmas tree — or a little bit of all three.

And this was when I looked up and saw him.

Just standing there.

Right by the cashier. Looking down into his wallet. Wearing jeans and a splattered T-shirt.

Matt.

I looked back down again, before looking up again, just to be sure. But I was already sure. He was buying a pack of cigarettes, pointing to the ones he wanted. He hadn't seen me yet.

"Oh, my God," I said. For a second, I

didn't think I had spoken out loud. I was pretty sure I hadn't spoken out loud. And I started looking all around me for a way out. He was between me and the exit. My only hope was hiding, quickly, behind the Slurpee counter.

But then he looked up at me — heard me, somehow — and I was still right where I'd been. In clear view.

At first, he didn't do anything. He just stood in place without saying a word. He had all the same things: light eyes, dark skin, girl-waist. His hair still flipped behind his ears — that awkward in-between flip that always seemed a little too business-man, and a little too NASCAR driver at the same time. It was my favorite part about him.

I wanted to be the first one to wave or do something. But I couldn't. My arms were too full of junk food. I couldn't even foresee a graceful way to put any of it down, or do anything at all.

"Hey," he called to me.

"Hey," I called back, trying to match his tone, his intonation, as if that would help something.

Then I watched as he took his change from the cashier and put his cigarettes in his pocket. I knew he wasn't going to yell or make a scene or do anything nasty, but I did think — truly — he was going to turn around right then, and walk right out the door. I thought he was going to walk right out the door as though he didn't know me.

But what he did instead was walk right toward me, carefully removing things from my arms, one item at a time, until he was carrying all of it.

"You've been smoking?" he said, motioning to the cigarettes.

I shook my head. "Just today. Not usually anymore."

He didn't look like he believed me. It was one of his funny things — one of his requests — even though he smoked, he never wanted me to. Even though he might have done things to hurt me, he never wanted me to hurt myself.

I cleared my throat. "Usually now I don't. I don't smoke now so much is . . . my point."

He nodded. "I saw Meryl earlier," he said.

"I know."

"She told you?" he said.

"She told me," I said.

We started walking to the counter, and he put everything down — beckoning to the cashier, who had disappeared somewhere in the middle of this. He took out his wallet to pay. As if this was what we did. As if we were there together.

The cashier handed him the bag of food, me the tray of drinks. We walked outside, stopping right in front of the store. I was worried I was going to cry. I was so worried I was going to cry. But I willed myself with everything I was not to. Not even to start. Because I knew — *I knew* — if I did, I'd never stop.

"Aren't you supposed to be at the rehearsal dinner at your folks' right now?" he said.

"Kind of," I said.

He nodded. "Do you have to go back?"

"Do you want me to go back?" I said.

"What's that?"

I closed my eyes, tears filling them up. I wasn't willing to ask for it again — what it was that I had started to ask for. But it turned out, I didn't have to ask again for anything. He reached out and touched my right cheek. First with the outsides of his fingers, then with the insides.

"Stay," he said.

For the first several weeks after I left Matt, I had the same recurring dream in which he would be sitting on a stool at the coffee shop near his parents' home in Maine, drinking a Dr Pepper, a large cup of coffee. This was the whole dream. Nothing else would happen. No one would talk to him, the coffee wouldn't spill, he wouldn't stand up or leave. It took me a while to figure out that I probably kept having the dream because this was the last thing I was sure Matt had done. I knew he had gone on to his parents' (what that arrival scene looked like, I couldn't imagine), and I knew he had, at one point over the remainder of that weekend, gone to that coffee shop and ordered his usual drinks. I could be sure of it. And I must have wanted to hold on to it, that one last thing I knew about him without question. The one last piece of knowledge that made him mine.

After we walked out of the 7-Eleven, the dream came back to me in full force, almost as if it were more real — more actual — than what was happening now. This — the walking to the car to tell Justin what was going on, that I'd call him tomorrow; the walking back quickly to where Matt was waiting for me — had become the dream, and it was like, without knowing it, someone had slipped me one drink too many. Suddenly the world had become hazy, slow-moving, everything appearing to me in faded, incomplete shapes.

But I followed Matt across the street anyway, in my somewhat stupefied state, to the one lone bench down behind the train station. The bench looked out on this great, misplaced waterfall, which ran into a river I didn't know the name of. A long row of rocks filled up on each side of it. Lots of woods and trees. It was like walking out of suburbia and into the middle of nowhere for a quarter of a mile or so.

We took a seat on the bench, a small space between us, and started to try to talk. I wasn't even sure how. I really didn't want to say the wrong thing to him. There seemed to be no safe territory. I doubted Matt wanted to talk about my leaving him that morning. I was scared of discussing that too, scared that he'd get mad and walk away and leave me alone here, which maybe I deserved. But I also didn't want to cover the time since. What was I going to say, anyway? I didn't want to tell him I was still living in Narragansett. I was afraid he'd misunderstand. And I was equally afraid he'd understand exactly.

"So I started playing ice hockey again," Matt said. "Up in Katonah actually.

There's this intramural team. We head up there every Saturday morning. Nine a.m. The goalie's a woman. Her name's Betty Lou. She just turned seventy-three."

"And she's good?"

"She can kick my ass."

I shook my head. "You're making this up."

"Scout's honor," he said, raising his hand.

"So that's what you're doing home this weekend? Celebrating Betty Lou's latest birthday?"

"That," he said. "And helping my parents get ready to move." I must have looked at him disbelievingly because he kept talking. "They're moving to Maine full-time. They like it better there anyway. So . . . I helped them repaint the downstairs, and they needed me to pack up whatever of my belongings I don't want left behind, and they're getting the hell out of Dodge." He lit a cigarette, and offered me the pack.

I shook my head, and he nodded, taking a drag. He did it in that way, though, blowing the smoke out the side, the way he used to, when he was nervous about telling me something. Which is why I'm not sure why I was surprised when he did.

"I'm actually thinking about moving too," he said. "I'm supposed to move. I'm supposed to go to Paris."

"Paris?" I looked at him. "As in France?"

"As in France."

I looked away from him, and then straight ahead at the waterfall. The water was doing the heavy lapping farthest away from us, vanishing over the bend. Unbelievable. He could have said anywhere else in the world, and he wouldn't have conjured up inside of me everything I was feeling now. How could I help but think of that trip to Paris that Matt and I had gone on together? And of course, the trip we *didn't* take all those years later, after we'd gotten engaged?

I cleared my throat. Matt hated Paris. Or at least didn't like it. If there were anything I didn't have a question about, it was that. Which let me know the first thing I didn't want to know, sitting here with him tonight. Someone was making the choice *now* for him.

"What she's doing in Paris?" I asked. "Your girlfriend?"

"My girlfriend?"

Who was it that said you should never ask a question unless you're ready to hear the answer? Was that just a Josh-ism too? I still was having too much trouble listening to it.

"Yes."

He smiled at me. "Well, my *ex*-girl-friend, Lily, was just transferred to her firm's Paris office," he said. "She's a tax attorney."

And he stopped there, not saying the rest of it. But I could start to hear it anyway: Matt getting a great job at a small French architecture firm, his first well-deserved break. He would start to love the city, explain to me one day that he just hadn't understood it before, but how, now, he was going to every small alley-café, every out-of-the-way gallery. How, tramping down the streets late at night, he found the hidden chapel behind the Champs-Elysées where the symphony practiced at midnight on Tuesdays, the front pews always empty.

Matt stubbed out his cigarette on the ground beneath the bench, clearing his throat while he did it. I stared at the cigarette. It was sinking in the ground, which was wet from the water, full of little puddles of mud.

"But it's my son I'm talking about," he said. "He's the reason that I'm trying to go there now."

I was sure I'd heard him wrong. "What?"

He nodded.

"I don't know what to say," I whispered. And I didn't. I started doing admittedly faulty math in my head, trying to figure the dates out. His son would be what now? *Could* be what? Two if he started seeing Lawyer Lily right after us. His son could be as old as two years old. "Do you have a picture?"

He felt around in his pocketless T-shirt, his empty jeans. "Not on me, I don't think," he said.

But it didn't matter anyway. The little boy was all I could see now. This sweet little baby. Matt's eyes and coloring. Someone else's nose and chin and long fingers. Someone else's lips.

"His name's Nathaniel."

"After your . . . grandfather?"

"Her father, actually. Her father had that name too. He died right before Nate was born last year."

I held my hand above my chest, staring at him. I thought it would suffocate me — my heart — it was beating so fast out of me. Matt was someone's father now. He had become someone's father. All these images of him came into mind: walking in the park, changing a diaper, standing cribside. Someone needed him for these most basic things, and I knew he was doing them, giving all he could. But the weirdest part was that he was looking at me so apprehensively, so carefully, like that wasn't the trick of it — of what he had to say to me. Like there was still more to come.

"Matt, I feel like I should be saying more, but it's just so much," I said, hoping there wasn't more, hoping I was wrong. "From ice hockey to Nathaniel in under five minutes."

"I'm sorry," he said.

"No." I reached out and touched his arm. It was the first time I had touched him. "Don't be. I think that's how it happens."

He looked down at my hand on his arm, before looking back up at me, meeting my eyes. I followed his eyes with mine, wanting to say something else. But before I could, he did. "Then forgive me," he said. "From going from there to this."

And he kissed me. He just leaned in and — just like that. It was so soft that I almost missed it. So soft and scared and light. There was no time to argue with it, almost no time to really even feel it.

As he pulled away, I felt stuck in place. My face still next to his. I couldn't seem to move.

"I'm sorry," he said.

"For which part?" I said. His breath right near my neck. His breath still a little too near.

"You should know," he said. "You're the reason I came home this weekend. You're the reason I'm here. I read your brother's wedding announcement in the paper, and I thought, I'll go home. I won't go find her, but at least I'll go home. And if I see her, I was supposed to see her. If I see her, I'll figure out a way to say what I want to say."

I was waiting to hear the rest of it — what he thought he was supposed to say — but it was like I was hearing just the beginning again and again. *You're the reason I came home.*

I moved closer to him.

"It all sounds better in my head," he said. "I love Lily. She gave me Nathaniel. I can't be sorry about that. But it's just not the same. With her or with anyone else. Things just aren't the same as they were with us." He paused. "When things were good with us, they were so good. Don't you think? Everything else just feels . . . less honest or something."

I tried to think of what to say back. I felt like I should say something back, if for nothing else than because he had managed to do that thing that only he seemed to know how to do: say something that fit perfectly into an empty place inside me.

"And I know that I cut out on you at the end of things with us. I know I really stopped being there," he said. "But I had all this stuff going on, and I couldn't manage to talk to you. It was hard sometimes with you. I knew that you still wanted me there, but there was a disconnect between what you were feeling and what you showed you were feeling."

I nodded because I did know. I did know that. I felt myself disconnect when I got scared. I felt myself, in the most important ways, and at the very worst times, disappear. Wasn't that what my whole life was starting to become in a way? A great disappearing act? Even from myself?

"Matt," I said. "I want to say something about that day in the motel room. I am sorry for how I left. I shouldn't have done it like that, obviously. I guess that's very obvious. But the thing was, I knew if I didn't do it right then, literally, I wouldn't be able to ever. I loved you so much still, and I could feel it. I could feel that you had stopped."

He nodded. "I get that."

"Really?"

"No."

He smiled when he said it, but it was an angry smile. Then he shook his head, and looked down. He was staring at the branches on the water's edge. I knew he wanted to pick one up so he could have something to do with his hands. It was that or he'd take another cigarette. I bent down and handed him a branch.

"What's that?" he said. "A peace offering?"

I smiled. "If you'll take it. And if you'll tell me the truth." I cleared my throat, bracing myself against it — what I was about to ask. What I hadn't, just yet, given myself permission to ask. "Who was she?"

"Who was who?" he asked.

I took a deep breath. I had been too scared to ask then, too scared to even let myself know there was something to ask. But with everything that had been happening over the last couple of days, I didn't feel so scared anymore.

"The woman you were involved with," I said. "At the end of us, I mean. Was it Nathaniel's mom?"

He didn't say anything at first, but I could see in his eyes that he was thinking of what to say. I could see him trying to decide how to be most fair. He turned and looked out at the water, away from me, which was a dead giveaway that he didn't have any idea.

I tried to help. "It was someone else?" I said for him. "Besides her? Besides Lily, I mean?"

"It was someone else."

I didn't say anything.

"I didn't think you knew about her," he said. "Even when you left like that, I didn't think you did."

"I didn't," I said. Because even if in the back of mind it had been a possibility, I hadn't seen it — hadn't let myself see it — until right now, this very weekend, where all around me people were missing signals they weren't ready for yet themselves.

He turned back to me. "I don't know what to say to you about it now," he said. "Without sounding like a self-help book."

I smiled. "She wasn't the cause of things between us, she was the result? I know all that."

"Do you?"

I nodded. Because I did. Because someone else seemed to be the least of it, all this time later, if he still wanted to be sitting here with me. If he had been with someone or had almost been with someone — or I had left him, or almost left him — wasn't the more important point

245

that we came back to each other now? Wasn't that at least as important as the rest?

"I don't know how to tell you I want to try again. . . ."

"Slowly would be nice," I said.

He smiled at me. "I still have the engagement ring, you know," he said. "That you left behind. I've kept it at my parents' this whole time."

I'd always been superstitious about engagement rings in general, and that didn't change when Matt gave me one. I couldn't shake the feeling that instead of being a token of affection, engagement rings had turned into a twisted type of bragging rights, which was something I feared people were punished for. I knew how much I loved him, and hadn't been worried — at the time — how he felt about me. I didn't think we needed a ring to prove anything.

"I just figured you'd sell it back," I said. "You knew I didn't really want it in the first place."

He threw the branch far out into the waterfall — the branch I had given him. It hit with a *crisp, crisp*. Then it disappeared.

"I know," he said. "That's why I kept it."

It was exactly midnight when Matt dropped me at my parents' house. There were still a few cars on the block, but the caterer seemed to be all packed up. Most of the lights inside the house were off, and both flower buggies were gone. The event, from out here at least, looked as though it had wound down.

We sat outside for a while, staring at the house, as if something were going to change — as if something were going to sneak out and surprise us, interrupt us. Or maybe that was just me. Maybe Matt was waiting for something else.

When nothing happened, we made plans to meet late tomorrow night — midnight, post-wedding — at the diner on Central Avenue we'd always gone to, to talk some more there. To keep talking about all of this.

I didn't want to talk anymore tonight.

All I wanted tonight was for Matt to kiss me again. This I wanted maybe more than anything, but I was afraid to do it myself. I was afraid of what that would open up.

So instead I kept talking, probably more than either of us wanted me to, about the only thing I couldn't seem to stop talking about, especially when I didn't have an answer for it yet myself.

"One last question," I said. "You don't have to answer it if you don't want to, but . . . what was she like?"

"Who?"

I didn't say anything, waiting for him to figure it out himself.

He looked out at the street, and I followed his eyes — followed Matt's angle of it. The first time he'd ever driven me home, he'd sat here for a long time after I went inside. What was he thinking of then? It couldn't be how impossible it would all one day become for him, so impossible that he'd look to someone else to simplify it. To simplify it, and complicate it, and give him a way out.

"I'm not asking for the reason you think," I said. "I'm not being masochistic or anything. I'm just trying to understand."

"Understand what?"

I wasn't ready to answer him. I wasn't ready to tell him about what was going on with Josh. I didn't want everything in my life to be about Josh, but it seemed like it was somehow, until I could figure out a way to untangle it again.

"I don't know." He shrugged. "I guess she was a little like you, actually. She was wacky and graceful and really smart. Well, maybe the graceful part isn't that much like you."

"Thanks a lot."

"No, she was just this person who made me feel good. What I remember about her most was that she had this weird obsessive-compulsive thing when she could only go to sleep if the clock was on certain numbers. I liked that for some reason. I liked waiting up with her when the time was coming out all wrong."

"Okay, this game is over," I said. "Not a good idea. Not a very smart game to play."

He put his hands on the steering wheel, and turned and looked at me — really looked at me.

"The point is that it was a mistake. And I'm not saying that to be nice. I'm not saying it for anything except that I'm telling the truth. I've thought about it a lot since then. And I've always been sorry that

I stepped outside of us like that. It was the only time. I guess that doesn't matter much. But whatever questions I was hoping to answer, Em, she didn't change the most basic part. Which was that I loved you."

If it weren't all so unfunny, I would have started laughing. I would have started laughing right then because this was the absolute most he'd ever said to me at one time. Why was that how it worked? Why could we say more to each other when it counted less?

I looked down at my hands. "The thing is that I think that Josh may be ruining things for himself, and I'm just not sure how to help him."

"Things with Meryl?"

"And Elizabeth."

"And Elizabeth." He nodded, taking this in. "Wow. Well, I don't know. But maybe it's not your job to help him."

"It feels like it is."

"I can understand that. But if it makes you feel any better, he probably already knows what he's going to do. I mean, in terms of the two of them, even if he hasn't said it out loud yet. He knows which way he has to go. He is probably just figuring out how to make himself do it."

I looked over at him. "Did you know?"

He nodded slowly. "I was going to marry you," he said. "There was no question. That's what I was going to do."

I didn't say anything, but I felt this incredible relief at hearing him say it — and then, almost simultaneously, this incredible sadness. If things were eventually going to work out, did it matter how you got there? Didn't it ultimately just matter that you got the ending you wanted?

"You know the weirdest part? I told her right before we left for Maine that weekend. That last weekend. I told her it was over, for good."

I tried to take this in, what I had done that weekend — that night in the hotel room — just at the moment, it seemed, before he came back to me. Was it really true that he would have, if I had let him? It didn't seem possible — and seemed completely possible — that I had needed to wait just one night more.

"Well, that just seems like the most unfair part," I said.

"To whom?"

"Everyone."

He smiled, and I smiled back. It was weird because — while I did it — I felt myself taking a snapshot of the way he looked right then, trying hard to hold it, imprint it really, so I could lock it in. Then I leaned all the way across him, turning the ignition back on for him.

"That's it?" he said. "You're done with me?"

I nodded. "For tonight," I said, even though what part of me was thinking was, Never. I will never be done with you, Matt. I will never be able to think about you and hear about you and not totally — totally — miss you.

"You are going to think about it though, right, Emmy? What we talked about. You'll give it some real thought?" he said.

There was a sense of desperation in his eyes that I didn't recognize, and I wondered what had happened to him in the last three years to put it in there. Or if I had done it, in my leaving. A small piece of me couldn't help but think we were sitting here together now — that he was so sure *now* — because I'd left. That he needed to get me back, so he'd know he still could. I was hoping that wasn't true, or at least not all that was true. I was also hoping that I wasn't right that if I said yes to him, his need would disappear. He would be the one deciding he didn't need this anymore.

"Of course I'll think about it," I said.

And then, for the first time in a long time, I did what I wanted to do. I leaned in and kissed him. It was me who kissed him this time, longer than before, and like I meant it. His lips felt different than I remembered, though, but I knew in a minute, it would be erased. In a minute, if I let it, it would feel the same as it always had.

I got out of the car and leaned down — my face inside the open passenger-side window.

He leaned over and touched it. "If you're going to be late or something, you'll call me?" he said. "You won't keep me waiting, right?"

"I won't," I said. I leaned in closer, that much closer into his hands. "I'll be there."

The first wedding superstition I remember learning about — during my own engagement, actually — was the one that said the bride and groom shouldn't see each other from midnight on, the night before their wedding. Matt had been the one to explain the history of it to me. He had come home with information about it, I think, in his bid to convince me to let him have his bachelor party the night before we were supposed to get married. Apparently, though, the reason the bride and groom were supposed to be separated the night before the wedding was that this was the night the bride stopped being a girl. In fact, ancient Greeks had this tradition of taking away all of the bride's old toys and belongings — even cutting off her hair if it were long — stripping her of everything that didn't have to do with her future life as someone's wife. What was the groom supposed to be doing during this time? Whatever he wanted.

This was what Josh was doing: sitting in the emptied-out rehearsal dinner tent all alone. The waiters, the guests, our family — they had all gone. It was just Josh sitting there at one of the remaining tables, a tablecloth still on it, one candle lit in the center, nothing else.

I walked toward him. He was staring down at his watch. He didn't look up from it even as I got closer.

"Twelve oh-two," he said, eyes still on his wrist, touching the watch's face. "Twelve oh-two. And . . . nineteen seconds."

"Officially your wedding day," I said.

"Officially my wedding day." He looked up at me, tried to give me a smile. It wasn't a successful effort.

I sat down across from him, carefully, not because I was afraid he'd tell me to go away, but because I was just starting to realize that there were several ways to stay with someone. And, depending on what I did, Josh might tell me everything, or we would get nowhere again.

"You missed Meryl's parents' speech," he said after a few minutes. "They were talking about commitment. They were talking about how they knew it the first time they met me. How they had that type of feeling about me. Someone who would do the right thing. Someone who would never let their daughter down."

"I'm sorry I left," I said.

He shook his head. "It was like her father was daring me. I swear to God. That's what it was like."

"I'm sure he wasn't daring you, Josh," I said.

"How can you be sure?"

"Because I'm imagining he wouldn't think he needed to." He looked at me, but didn't say anything. I cleared my throat. "Are you feeling better about things? Did you sit down and talk to Meryl?"

Josh moved the lit candle toward him, starting to run his fingers along the edges — in and out of the heat. "She went back to the city before I could."

He said it so softly, I thought, at first, I misunderstood. But inside, I knew I hadn't.

I felt something rising up in me, tried to push it down. It was a hectic night. I could try to understand that. Josh could still talk to her in the morning. But it did feel important to me that he talk to her, one way or the other. Only, I needed to ask myself: why did I want him to talk to her so badly?

Was is it just because I thought he needed to be honest about everything? Or was it something else too? After today, wasn't at least part of me rooting for Elizabeth? And for Grace? For the Josh I'd seen around them?

"I ran into Matt tonight," I said.

Josh looked up at me. "What?"

"For some reason, when Meryl told me she ran into him, I assumed it was in the city." I shrugged. "But it was here. She ran into him here. And, are you ready for this? He has a child. A thirteen-month-old son. Can you believe that? Matt is someone's father."

Josh didn't say anything, but he looked down too quickly. He started focusing again on the candle. Balling up the hot wax.

"Josh, you didn't know, did you?"

He looked back up at me, his eyes confirming his answer even before he confirmed it out loud. I felt my whole body drop, fall completely into itself. He had known that. He had known something so huge about Matt, and had not needed to tell me? I felt it all going — my ability to handle any of this.

"I heard something about it when I was in town a few months ago for Meryl's and my engagement party. Someone had heard from someone who said they had heard from his mother. Or something like that. I don't even know. But I wasn't a hundred percent sure, and I didn't want to upset you. I didn't want to upset you unless I confirmed it myself."

"No, I can see how this is much better. I'm much happier that I found out this way. Really."

"I'm sorry," he said.

But his words meant nothing to me — not after everything I had put myself through for him this weekend. I felt myself getting really angry. I didn't know how to stop it. I didn't know how to halt what was coming next.

I pulled the candle away from him. It was a silly thing to do, but it was all I had right then. So I took it, and put it down in front of me, daring him to take it back again.

He looked down at his empty hands, then looked over at me. "Emmy, I really can't do this right now, okay? We can deal with it tomorrow if you want. For as long as you want. Or . . . I don't know. I just can't talk about it now."

"Well, that's the whole problem, Josh, isn't it?" I said. "You're totally unwilling to talk about anything. Because you think that once you say it out loud, it becomes a little too true."

His look of irritated pity switched before my eyes to something closer to mine — something also displaying anger. "Why?" he said. "Because I didn't tell you something about Matt the second I heard it? When I didn't have confirmation that it was true? He's not even in your life anymore."

Not in my life anymore. The year Matt's brother had turned three, we'd had a birthday dinner for him in the city: pizza and ice cream sundaes and bottomless cream sodas. We put up a Superman tent up in the living room and let him stay up as late as he wanted and watch all his favorite cartoons. When he finally fell asleep — Matt in a sleeping bag on one side of him, me on the other — Matt turned toward me and said, "Isn't it amazing? You'll have known him his entire life." My entire life. Tonight he was offering it to me again.

I turned away from Josh now. "You don't know what you're talking about," I said.

"Really? I know how long it's been already. I know you keep asking these fishermen women to tell you how to do it."

"Tell me how to do what?"

"Wait long enough. For Matt to come back."

He looked at me so intensely that it was all I could do to look back at him, to try to stand my ground. But my burning desire to tell him that Matt had, in a way, come back to me made me wonder if he did know. It made me wonder what I wasn't seeing about my own life. What I really didn't want to see, at all.

"You don't even want to try to understand," he said. "What I'm going through now."

"Maybe that's true," I said.

And maybe I didn't. I didn't, for sure, want to get into what Berringer had said to me earlier about not supporting Josh, but as soon as Josh said I wasn't trying to understand him, Berringer's voice came ringing back in my ears. I didn't want to talk about — let alone think about — how much Berringer's opinion was affecting me. And I certainly didn't want to think about how much I hadn't liked seeing him with Celia. The other truth was that I felt done trying to understand what Josh was doing because he wasn't *doing* anything. He was just going to keep worrying about all of this until the decision was made for him, until he walked down the aisle, and let someone else tell him how he was going to be spending his life. But, I saw now, even that wouldn't be about making a choice. It would be about taking the path of least resistance, which was a totally different thing.

"You're just so mad at me, Emmy," Josh said, misunderstanding my look. "You won't even see that I'm confused. I'm just confused about what the right thing to do is. Can't you understand that at all?"

I shook my head. How could I tell him what I really thought? That, inside, he knew exactly how this was going to play out? He knew it exactly, but he just kept doing what he wanted to anyway, so he could keep everyone in, keep them hoping.

But he was going to marry Meryl. Or he would have done something else. He would have done something else a long time ago. It was the most unfair and wrong way to go about it that I could think of.

"The thing I don't get, Josh," I said, "is what's so great about you? What's so great about you that both these women should want to be with you regardless of what you've done? What makes you so special?"

He leaned toward me, and, for a second,

I really thought he was going to knock the candle off the table — my brother, who had never so much as jokingly slapped me growing up. But instead he just stayed leaning in, toward me.

"You want to know a secret? Nothing's so special about me," he said. "That's what they'd both find out. They're both better than me. I haven't done anything yet to deserve either one of them."

I leaned in too. "Then why don't you do something now?"

Josh kept looking at me, but he didn't say anything. He didn't say that I was right — that he wasn't going to marry Meryl, or that Elizabeth and Grace were going to be okay either way. He didn't tell me that love fell second to commitment, sometimes, if for no other reason than people were too scared to let things be any other way. That they had trouble even beginning to know how to be so honest.

He didn't tell me this — he didn't tell me anything — in part because, before he could, out of the shadows, came Dr. Moynihan-Richards. He was holding a package from CVS Pharmacy — the only all-night drugstore anywhere in town. He was still wearing his suit.

Josh stood up, smoothing out his tie as if

this were the main problem. "Dr. Richards," he said. "I had no idea you were there."

"Clearly," he said. And walked away.

I looked up at Josh in disbelief. He was looking toward where Meryl's father had just been. I knew he was trying to decide whether to go after him. But what was he going to say anyway? What was there to say even if he caught up to him, and could — somehow — convince him to listen for a second? *I really do love your daughter, sir, but I can't quite be sure if she's the best person for me to spend the rest of my life with.*

"Josh," I said, "I had no idea he was standing there. You don't think he heard us, do you?"

"The part where you were yelling? Um . . . yeah. I think he may have heard that part."

I didn't know what to say. I watched him sit back down, pull the tablecloth back toward him. It knocked the candle and remaining flowers off the table. It knocked away a stranded fork, the wet-naps.

"This is fucking great."

I leaned across the table toward him. "Listen to me, okay? He couldn't have known what we were talking about. Not really. You can make something up if it comes to that."

He looked over at me, but it was like he didn't see me. Like he was trying to figure out who I even was, really. He had never looked at me like that before. It made me feel scared.

"Look, Emmy," he said. "I don't think I want to be around you very much right now."

"Well, I don't want to be around you right now either," I said, and with that, I stood up.

And I left him there. For the first time, maybe ever, I left my brother behind. I knew he would just keep sitting there in our parents' backyard, in his vacated rehearsal dinner tent — the tablecloth bunched up, red table exposed beneath it — at a total loss.

I knew Dr. Moynihan-Richards was still out there, somewhere, in the shadows, or that he was on his way back into the basement to share his information. I knew that in a minute or two, Josh would start to cry.

I didn't turn around.

part four

Maybe I'm wrong, but there does seem to be something buzzing around in the air on wedding days, this all-encompassing fragrant thing that gets caught there the same way it does on Christmas or on a snow day. The second snow day in a row when you're ten years old, say, and, even inside, everything is all frosty and hidden, the static creeping up from the radio in the kitchen, the broadcaster just about to tell you the very best news you could ever imagine hearing. You almost can't believe it. And yet somehow, instinctively, you've been waiting for it.

Three of the happiest wives — Nancy #1, Josie #3, and Jill #4 — had all said they'd had a version of this feeling on their wedding days. And even Kristie #2, who was currently in the middle of a divorce, smiled when she remembered feeling certainty on her wedding day. "We got married at Pete's friend's place on Block Island," she said. "And even now, I know I was absolutely supposed to marry him that morning. I was supposed to become his wife."

When I opened my eyes that morning of Meryl and Josh's wedding, this was the first thing I felt — that a wedding was going to happen today, that it absolutely would (which meant it should), and that everything was going to move forward as planned. It was bizarre to me that this was my gut reaction.

And yet, for that first seemingly honest minute after I awoke, I got to believe that this feeling cemented something — that any doubts I had been having about whether or not they should get married had turned out to be misguided. For that first minute, it didn't seem to matter much what had happened yesterday. All of it — the farm and Elizabeth and even Grace — felt like a dream. Maybe I had dreamed it. Because a wedding was going to take place today. I was sure of it. I was so sure of it that I didn't want to think about the rest of it, and it was the only time since Friday night, since sitting with Josh at the fireworks, that this felt like the right move. Maybe it would all die, disappear somehow, under the importance of what was about to happen.

Then, as if in a rush, I started feeling around for something else that was going on inside me — the stirring up in my stomach — and I remembered. I got to remember again. Matt. Seeing Matt. The two of us sitting together by the waterfall. What was said.

I ran my finger over my lower lip, replaying the scene in my head, slower this time, looking for hints in it. Not so much as to what I should do — which I still couldn't begin to think about — but what had been done. Was Matt a stranger to me now? Was he anything close to the version of him that had been living in my head — my heart — for the last several years? Which version was I really holding on to? I wasn't sure I could formulate anything resembling a real answer. All I knew was that his coming back to me felt so different than I'd imagined it feeling. There wasn't that element of relief I'd anticipated. It was more complicated than that, less precise. And I didn't know for certain what had inspired it — his decision to want to try again. But part of me knew him, knew him still, and understood that despite what he had told me, despite his saying that nothing else made him as happy as we had made him, he was also just scared. I had seen it in his eyes. He was scared to go to Paris, scared to take this next big step alone, and he could be sure I would back him up there. What would happen, though, when Paris wasn't scary anymore? Would he still be so sure that I was the one he wanted to be with, or would other things — other people — again hold more interest? Would I have to feel again like his love could disappear at any time?

I got out of bed, heading straight to Josh's room, but he wasn't in there. The bed was already made, the window wide open. If he had even slept in there at all, he was already up and gone.

I rubbed my eyes, trying to really wake myself up, and moved over to the window. Outside was all sun: the ground dark and hot, everything tinted red. It wasn't even nine, and it was burning out. I didn't have to turn on the radio to hear for sure what everyone had been saying. A summer heat wave was raging. Heat already here, and getting stronger. Stay inside unless you really have to be somewhere. Stay inside with the air conditioner on until this whole thing passes us by.

It gave me hope.

The wedding was scheduled for four, but the house was already busy with all of it. I could hear my mother downstairs — sausage frying, the phone ringing. I went down into the kitchen to find my mother by the stove, cooking two large griddles' worth of pancakes, fresh blueberries melting into them, bananas already in the mix.

"Don't tell me no one's going to eat this," she said as I sat down on the stool, leaning my elbows on the counter.

"I'm going to eat it," I said.

She turned and looked at me, the spatula in her hand. "I love you," she said. "Go put some socks on."

"It's a million degrees outside," I said.

"I don't care. Sickness comes in through the feet."

She put the spatula down and reached into the cabinet under the sink, emerging with a pair of clean, white tennis socks wrapped in plastic. You would think she had had to be kidding, but of course, she wasn't. She looked at me imploringly until I reached over and took the socks from her. Then she went back to her pancakes, flipping the soft batter over.

"Have you ever heard of using peanut butter to fry something instead of oil? It's really good. It gives it a sweet taste."

"Can we skip the crazy talk this morning?" she asked, not turning around, just motioning with the spatula for me to cover my feet.

I did what I was told, pulling the first sock on.

"So," she said, "someone left the dinner a little early last night, yes? Tell me. Do we like Mr. Silverman?"

"*We* are too busy thinking about running into Matt."

She turned and looked at me carefully. "Really?"

I nodded. "At the 7-Eleven last night," I said. "Kind of near the Slurpee machine. I tried to hide, but, you know I tend to be a little less than quick on my feet."

She leaned across the counter, reaching for my hand, uncharacteristically not saying anything, which was a good thing. Because if she asked even one other question, I'd have to tell her about his son. I'd have to tell her my heart still seized up at the sight of him, and that I was supposed to see him again tonight. Go through it again tonight. I'd have to tell her the whole story, which I couldn't begin to get a handle on yet.

"He's moving to Paris in a couple of

weeks," I offered instead. "He's looking for a job there now."

Her eyes stared back at me, small and worried. It was the look she reserved for when she was too worried to even say she was worried. I hated seeing it. I hated doing anything but making her happy. "I'm okay, Mom," I said. "Really. I just wanted you to know what was going on."

"Which is what?"

I thought of what Matt had said yesterday about wanting me with him, how that, again, could actually be possible. Maybe more possible than ever, more possible than it even was years ago, because he was ready for it too. He was certain.

"Nothing," I said.

She nodded, even though I knew she didn't believe me. Even though I could feel her wanting to say something else. Only before she could even decide whether to, we were interrupted by my ringing telephone. MERYL. Cell.

She looked down at the caller ID so she could see too. "You're not going to get that?"

"I'm getting it," I said. But I didn't make a move to yet, trying to decide what I could say to Meryl to sound the most like myself — the most like a version of myself she'd recognize.

So my mother did it for me. "She's right here, love," she said to Meryl, looking at me. "I'll hand you over."

I took the phone reluctantly, trying to smile at her as I did, looking totally unsuspicious. I was fairly sure I hadn't pulled it off. But she returned to the stove anyway, just as I put the phone to my ear.

"Hey there," I said into the receiver. "How's the bride?"

"Good," Meryl said.

But her voice came out quiet, sad, as if she were anything but. In the sound of it, the image of Dr. Moynihan-Richards standing in the dark came swimming back to me. Maybe he'd told her what he heard. Maybe she was sad because she now knew.

"Bess just planned this awful beauty day for me, at the hotel pre-wedding," she said. "Like a really bad surprise. Or just her attempt to distract me from the fact that it's two million degrees outside." She paused. "I was hoping you'd come in and keep me company."

I looked at the clock. It was only 9:45. The last thing I wanted to do was spend the entire day with Meryl — in case everything came up, or in case nothing did. Either way I'd feel terrible. I wasn't the one being dishonest with Meryl. Only now I was the one being dishonest with Meryl.

"What time were you thinking?" I asked.

"How's twenty minutes ago?"

I looked in the direction of the doorway, as if Josh was going to appear and tell me what do. But I knew what he'd want me to do. He'd want me to go. "I'm on my way," I said.

My mother watched as I hung up the phone. "And that's the end of you?" I nodded. "Good. It will give me more time to work on my this-is-what-it-all-means speech," she said.

"You think I need one of those speeches?" I said.

"I think several people around here need one of those speeches," she said.

I looked down at the list she'd written on the countertop notepad: CALL 4 EXTRA FLOWERS, BAND CHECK-IN AT 2:30 [Sam], SMALL PRESENT FOR BESS, MERYL'S GARTER, COORDINATE AIRPORT PICK-UPS [Sam], EMMY'S VIDEOS TO HOTEL [Sam].

"What's this?" I said, running my finger over VIDEOS TO HOTEL.

"Oh, I thought it would be fun to watch them tonight after the wedding. We have the suite there, and we can order in pop-corn and relax. Have a little Emmy time before you leave us again."

Leave, again. I should have felt a relief just at the words — at getting out of this situation where things, major things, seemed to be changing every second. But I didn't feel relief. If it made me feel any-thing — the thought of going back to quiet Rhode Island, that empty, peaceful house — it made me feel lonely. Before I could argue, though, explain that I didn't *have* to leave immediately, she stopped me.

"Your dad already has them in the car," she said, shaking her head. "Under the air conditioner, of course. We're looking for-ward to it. It's already done."

I squeezed her arm. "Thank you, Mom."

She smiled. "Don't thank us. Thank your friend Berringer."

"Berringer?"

"It was his suggestion that we all watch the videos tonight. He mentioned it when he came to pick up your brother for a morning jog. In this heat, they went. Does that seem like a good idea?"

She shook her head, and I started to walk out of the kitchen, thinking about Berringer, how he had done that, how he cared enough that he wanted to not just hear what I was doing, but see exactly what I was doing.

"Is there something you want me to tell him for you?" she said, stopping me. "Your brother, I mean. I don't think they'll be back before you leave."

"Like what?"

"I don't know," she said, but she was looking at me like she did already.

"How did he seem this morning, Mom?" It was the closest I'd come to acknowledging that something was wrong.

She smiled at me. "What are you looking for me to say, Emmy? Like a man who's about to get married?"

My maid-of-honor dress — the long and strappy number — was being *protected* by a thin, silver garment bag, which actually added a strange light to the dress, making it look closer to sheer. But it was still a bridesmaid dress, and the worst kind of bridesmaid dress — the one the bride would try to convince you that you could wear again. To a southern wedding, maybe, or the Kentucky Derby. Who was going to those places anytime soon? And how was this dress the answer to a future trip? I wasn't all that thrilled about wearing it even this time. Long dresses like this gave all my curves their chance to shine, and not in a good way.

While a *nice* boyfriend might say it was a good look for me, a more honest one would admit that straight and sheer like this made me look a little un-thin. But at this point I was so full of guilt about everything I knew and everything I couldn't do that I was anxious to wear this dress if it could make everything okay for Meryl — if it could somehow make yesterday and Elizabeth and Grace keep feeling far away. Not because I wanted to forget them, but because I wasn't sure how I could go on remembering them, and ever forgive Josh. In this, I knew Josh and I were still the same. I knew he wanted to forget them too — had probably spent years trying to do so — so he could start to forgive himself. How had that worked out for him?

I carried the dress and the rest of my belongings back through the bushes over to the Wademans', where June's Volvo was waiting for me. I got in, squeezing into the already overcrowded backseat my garment bag and purse and the key chain I'd bought for Meryl in Newport last week. This had been my plan for my toast. To give Meryl the key chain with just one key on it and to tell her the story about Josh and me and our key collection. To say that it was so nice that now he had the one key that could open any door. It was corny, I knew, but I also thought they'd love it. Meryl and Josh. And this had seemed like the point. Now it seemed like I needed a new plan, a more honest one.

I backed the car out of the parking spot quickly, heading for the Hutch. To get there, I had to pass by the turnoff for Matt's street, which was something I couldn't bear doing right then.

"He has a *son.*" I said it first in my head — then out loud to myself, so I'd have to hear it, this time, what it really meant. Any woman he was with now would assume that was the reason she didn't have his full attention. That the child was the reason. That he was the main reason there was just a piece of Matt she didn't have. And she'd be able to forgive it. His absence.

When I hit the highway, I turned on the radio just in time to hear a local DJ talking about the weather today. "If it gets any hotter out there," he said, "I can scramble an egg on my own forehead."

"God knows you have enough grease on that skin of yours," the sidekick answered him.

Gross. I was sick of hearing these weather reports. I was sick of hearing about records. I changed the station. Air Supply. It wasn't the song "Making Love Out of Nothing at All," it was the other one by them that everyone knew. The one that ended well. Josh and Meryl's wedding song. It seemed like hearing it signified something, but I didn't know what. Except a reminder that Air Supply sucked.

My cell phone rang in the glove compartment. I reached for it, grabbing it on the third ring. JAMES BERRINGER. James Berringer? I hadn't put his number there — had never in my life even called him James.

"Hello?" I said, confused.

"Hello yourself," he said.

I double-checked the caller ID — then triple-checked it — as if his voice hadn't been enough to make me sure that it was, in fact, him. "How did your number get stored in my phone?"

"I put it there after you took off last night."

"You put it there last night?"

"Are you going to repeat everything I say?"

I didn't answer him, just waited for him to tell me what was going on. I couldn't picture it: Berringer huddled by the corner living room table, entering number after number, trying to figure out how my antiquated phone even managed to function in the first place.

"I wanted to make sure that we were okay," he said. "I hated that you got so mad at me last night."

"I didn't get *so* mad at you," I said. "And anyway, if you were so worried I was mad, weren't you worried I wouldn't pick up after knowing that it was you on the other end?"

"Maybe, but I still wanted you to have a choice in it. In whether to pick up."

"You're a weirdo," I said, but I was smiling as I said it, embarrassed, all of a sudden, as though he was going to catch me. As if he was going to be able to hear what was happening in my chest during this phone call, the speeding up of everything, the inner buzz, a little too much like happiness.

He cleared his throat. "So your brother was saying it turned out to be a long night for you."

I cleared mine back, which sounded more like a hiccup. I just didn't know how to answer him. I didn't want to talk about Matt. Not with Berringer. "So you and Josh actually did go running then?" I said. "I thought it was a cover and he'd taken off again. That he went back to Rhode Island or something."

"I don't think he's taking off again, Em," he said. "I think he's done taking off."

I tried to picture Elizabeth and Grace

having breakfast at their kitchen table. I couldn't really. I pictured them driving somewhere in that pickup truck, not talking to each other maybe yet, but listening to something on the radio: Grace singing along to it, Elizabeth watching her, making herself relax. However anyone wanted to look at this, Josh was taking off.

"Anyway, that's really not what I was calling to talk to you about," he said. "I want to know why you got so mad at me. And don't tell me you're not. Because you were, and I think I know why."

I took a deep breath in, not sure what Berringer thought he knew, but very certain I didn't want to hear it myself. Especially if it began and ended with him thinking I felt a certain way. I wasn't ready to think about that totally — whether or not he was there to watch me do it.

"Berringer, you know what? Whatever you think you know, I'm sure you're not right."

"That's a fairly broad statement," he said.

"Well, I'm on the highway," I said. "And driving someone else's overstuffed station wagon rather questionably. And running late. So less broad statements are going to have to wait. Unless you have an idea of something for me to say to Meryl, whom I can't so much manage to be around right now."

"I'm sorry about that," he said. And from the way he said it, I knew he was. I knew he was sorry, and I also knew he wanted to fix it for me, even if he couldn't. "Will it make you feel better to know it will pass? The weirdness you're feeling?"

It made me feel worse, actually, because I knew it was true. As much as I was living in these days now, it was *because* I was living in them. But soon other days would bank up, other things would come to my mind, and they would trump these private truths I had seen, for a minute, about how my brother wanted to live.

"You know what? We can talk about this all later," he said. "Are you driving safely?"

"Trying to," I said.

But there was something about the question that stopped me for a second. It made me think of Matt. With everything that had been said, Matt hadn't asked me a thing about what I was up to in Rhode Island. I hadn't really wanted him to, but still. I knew about his son and about France and even about his hockey team. But he had absolutely no idea about the documentary or the tackle shop or the 107 wives. He

284

had no idea about the sum total of what my life had become. And I knew he would say I didn't volunteer the information, which wasn't untrue. Still, shouldn't it have mattered enough to him to ask what was going on with me? Even if it didn't exactly have to do with him?

"Well. I'm sorry I made you feel bad," Berringer said. "For the record. I'd never want to do that."

I wasn't used to that — someone being honest with me, so naturally. It made me feel a little uncomfortable, mostly because I was so lousy at doing it myself. But it also made me feel something else, which I was starting to like.

"That's okay," I said. "For the record."

"Yeah?"

"Yeah."

"Then the rest can wait."

In the early 1930s — during the heart of the Great Depression, the country in absolute financial ruin — almost all of the major construction in New York City came to a total halt. Only two buildings that were supposed to go up during this time kept being built as planned. One of these was the Essex House. And everything about it seemed like a testimony to prove that. The entire building was a standing example to its own largeness, its inability to fall. When you walked in the lobby, even today, you were greeted by old-school mahogany pillars and chandeliers, jewelry cases full of silverware and intricate china every few steps. The floor shiny and marbleized. I'm not saying it was ugly, but everything was so severe, so intentional and heavy, that it felt, at the least, like something you were supposed to brace yourself against. What I noticed first, stumbling in with my garment bag and full arms, was that there was nothing alive to look at: no vases of fresh flowers, no large green plants. No fishbowl of fishes. It was the exact opposite of a place I'd envision for myself to get married in, the opposite of outside.

The man behind the reception desk was very unhappy about letting me upstairs, even after Meryl confirmed that I could come. I wasn't exactly sure why this was, but when he gave me a dirty look, I tried to give him one back. Really, I just ended up looking at myself in the mirror behind him: my hair toppled on top of my head, my tank top a little ripped around the edges. Too-long jeans.

How could I even blame him for thinking badly of me? Nothing about me said I belonged in this place. Nothing about me, I was starting to worry — on top of everything else I was managing to worry about — really said I belonged anywhere.

"Miss Mitchelson is in Suite 2401," the man said, pointing me toward the right bank of elevators. "Do you think you can remember that, or would you like me to write it down?"

"I can try," I said, and headed that way. But by the time I actually knocked on Meryl's door, it was after eleven. My knock nudged the door open, revealing that Meryl's pre-wedding beauty day suite wasn't a suite at all. It was more like an entire floor: twelve-foot balcony windows looking out over Central Park, three separate living rooms, shiny old paintings covering the walls.

I found Meryl in living room 2. She was sitting cross-legged in the center of the floor, three large fans swimming around her. There was a long wooden table, which I was assuming she'd pushed off to the side, fully covered with silver teakettle sets and bottles of champagne and platinum fresh fruit platters. Little bowls of small chocolate hearts.

"You just missed the manicurist," she said, holding up shiny white fingernails as proof. "And the psychic."

I walked over to her, slowly. The only makeup she'd had done besides her nails were her eyes, which — in contrast to her pale skin, her tightly pulled back hair — were so dark and sharp they were spiderlike. Even like this, she was absolutely more graceful than I could ever hope to be.

"Don't worry. I asked the manicurist to come back later," she said. "I figured you didn't need the psychic giving you any good news. Though he is quite famous, apparently. A regular fixture among the celebrity set, out in Hollywood."

I sat down across from her, the fans blowing me back. "The only psychic I've ever met came into the tackle shop right around Christmas last year. She told me I was going to fall in love four more times before I met the person I was supposed to be with," I said. "And she also said our eel was basically no good for catching any fish of substance."

"See? Who needs news like that?" Meryl said, smiling at me, and starting to look around the room. "I guess my mother wanted me to be enjoying this," she said. "With the whole bridal party. She forgot I wasn't having one. Changes things, huh?"

"Changes things," I said, and crawled over toward the table, reached up for one of the low-riding platters of fruit.

"The nice thing about your mom," she said as I crawled back toward her, "is that she's going to want to just keep you all for herself when you get married. It will end up being just you and her on a private boat, or in New Jersey somewhere. You won't have to deal with any of this."

"Yeah," I said. "That's really something to look forward to."

She laughed. "So did you have a chance to see Josh this morning before you left?"

"No, he went running."

"Oh."

"No, I mean he *literally* went running, right before I left. I don't know what they were thinking in this heat. But he was with Berringer. That was what they were doing together."

She nodded as though she hadn't needed the additional reassurance. And why would she have, really? There wasn't any reason: no clues about Elizabeth lying around, about where we'd been heading this time yesterday. It wasn't written on my head or anything. So I was only saying it for another reason, if I wanted to be honest. I was just saying it for myself.

I offered her a cantaloupe ball.

"No, thanks," she said.

"You sure?" I said. "They're good for you."

"Positive," she said.

I put one in my mouth and started to chew. "So what did this famous psychic tell you anyway? Anything good?"

"Well." She looked up toward the ceiling, thinking about it. "First he said I was destined for a lifetime of happiness. And one of incredible love. Then he said that he thought today was going to mark the new beginning of finding that love. As long as I could let myself see it that way."

I popped in another ball.

"I'm guessing that's supposed to be the tricky part of it, wouldn't you think?" she said.

I covered my mouth. "Definitely," I said.

And this was when she started to cry.

Often, I've wished this were a movie. Because if it were, in this next scene, Meryl would explain that her tears — which were growing louder and more unstoppable — were tears of confusion. That she was having real doubts about today. Did she really want to get married today, did she even remember the reasons she had chosen Josh, did she not love someone else, a little bit more too? And I would get to listen to her. I would get to listen while she explained she wanted things he didn't, things that he never really wanted to give her or share with her: a high-profile career, a permanent life in Los Angeles, the chance to travel around the world. Then she would hug me, and decide it was all okay. That it was better to know this now than ten years from now. And she'd wait for Josh to get here and they'd call the whole thing off and lock themselves in this fake bridal suite and have one last drink of fancy champagne before wishing each other well.

But this wasn't a movie. It was someone's life, and this woman whom I loved and who had watched me grow up and whom I'd been withholding from for the last seventy-two hours because I'd picked my brother over her — she was crying because she loved my brother, more than ever maybe, and because she knew that there was something very, very wrong between them.

"I'm sorry," she said. "The last thing I would want to do is put you in the middle of this. You know I wouldn't want to do that, right? You know I would never want that?"

We were sitting on the sofa now in living room 1, or really, I was sitting by her feet. Meryl was lying down in an attempt to force the tears upward — toward her forehead — not down her cheeks, where they were quickly creating makeup track marks down the sides of her face.

"Maybe the two of you just need to talk. If any two people should be talking here, it should be you two. Let me call him."

"No." She shook her head, tears spreading outward. "I don't want to hear anything he wants to tell me right now. I don't want to hear anything that he is going to use as an excuse, that's for sure."

I looked at her in total confusion. An excuse for what? For what he was feeling? It seemed to me that was the best possible thing she could hope for here — that any one of us could hope for. That someone would tell the truth.

Meryl blotted both of her eyes with a tissue, as she tried to get ahold of herself again.

Then she sat up. "I know, okay?" she said. "I know there was someone that last year he was in Boston. Of course I know that. He basically told me himself right after he came out to Los Angeles. He tried to make it sound like it had happened and it was over, but those things don't end. Even if he wasn't seeing her anymore, I knew it still mattered to him or he wouldn't have felt the need to tell me at all. How can he think I don't know that about him? I know everything about him."

"Then what are you doing here?" I said. But as soon as the words were out, I was sorry — sorry, and worried that they sounded too harsh. I hadn't meant them to sound that way. It just all seemed so much sadder to me, sitting here and listening to her. Everything about the promises that were about to be made today felt that much worse.

"It's just that things stop being that simple," she said. "I still believe I'm the person he's supposed to be with. Those first few years, Josh wanted to marry me any day of the week. I just had all these ideas in my head about waiting longer, or waiting until we were settled financially or something. You wait long enough, and it's harder for a guy to make a commitment. Not easier." She shrugged. "I think I waited too long. And I know you think I sound like an idiot now and I'm just making excuses. But I'm not going to be the one to call it off. If Josh wants that, he's going to have to do it. Because I can see it being right between us. I can see it turning out okay. More than okay. And if he didn't see that too, why would he be here?"

I shook my head. "He wouldn't," I said.

"That's right," she said. "He wouldn't."

She sat up taller, almost as if she'd reached a new resolution. And I wondered how many times she'd been in this position before. Knowing what she knew, and pushing it away. Waiting until she calmed down enough to keep going. To do what she thought she needed to do.

And then, all of a sudden, I wasn't only seeing her anymore. I was seeing myself also. All of this time, I had seen similarities between Josh and me, which was part of the reason that I felt so mad at him — so angry and upset thinking he was screwing up his life too. But similarities were right here as well. Between Meryl and me. If I had stayed with Matt, this could be my wedding day too. I could just as easily be the one pushing aside what I didn't want to know, so I could move toward where I wanted to be. With him.

In how many hours was I going to see Matt again? And, just like that, was I going to fall back in? What made me think it would be any different this time? Because he said so? Or because — still like Meryl — I wanted to believe what I needed to believe? That this time, he wouldn't stop loving me. He wouldn't start seeing someone else or get distant or disappear on me in all the ways that really mattered most. He wouldn't make it all about him.

Meryl started to stand up.

"How can I help you?" I said.

"I have to finish getting ready," she said. "I should go and start putting my dress on."

"There's about five million buttons in the back of it," she said, heading toward the bedroom. "Of the dress. It looks beautiful done up, but it's a total nightmare getting there. I'm going to need your help. It's a nightmare like you wouldn't believe."

I stood up to follow her. "Just show me what to do," I said.

Statistics from a ten-year Princeton University study on the nature of modern marriages and domestic partnerships indicate that over 75 percent of the time it is the woman who ends a marriage or a long-term living situation. The man may do something to make her want to leave — he may be unfaithful or lie to her or push her away — but ultimately, if she doesn't leave him, he will stay also. After time, he will want to work it out and be good to her again, and try to make things better. And if that's what the woman really wants — if she just stays still long enough — in the end, she'll get her wish. Psychologists who conducted the study said the reason for this was the same across the board: men don't want to be the bad guy. They don't want to make a mistake they can't unmake. They want, only, for someone else to decide.

I couldn't help but think of this while I

waited in the living room for Meryl to finish getting ready. Wasn't that precisely what was going on here, after all? She had waited it out, and she and Josh had made it. They were about to more than make it, actually, embarking on the next big step together.

Meryl called out to me, for the third time, that she needed just a couple more minutes.

"I'm getting nervous to show you," she said.

"Maybe that means you're supposed to," I said.

I had no idea if this was true, but it sounded good. And I was getting a little tired of sitting in the living room by myself. I had turned all the fans off so they wouldn't blow on her, but even with the air-conditioning set on full blast, it wasn't exactly comfortable in there — the air more milky-warm than anything else. I was ready to go downstairs, where Bess and my mom and Mrs. Moynihan-Richards were waiting, and where, hopefully, everything was a little cooler.

I went into the kitchen to get our bouquets out of the refrigerator: small white lilies for me, one long orchid for Meryl. It was then — a bouquet in each hand — that

I heard a knock on the suite door. I assumed it was Bess, who I could only imagine didn't at all like being relegated to the downstairs waiting area for so long.

But when I got to the door, standing there before me with his tuxedo on — his white bowtie already tied around his neck — was Josh.

"It's you," I said in disbelief.

"It's me." He smiled down at me, putting his hand on my shoulder tentatively. He had a line of small sweat beads right above his mouth, running slowly down the sides of his face. "You look nice," he said, which I knew was also his way of saying we were okay.

In spite of everything — or maybe because of it — I couldn't ever remember feeling so relieved. I smiled at him, a genuine smile, and told him that he did too. I didn't say anything about the sweat on his face.

I did feel compelled to say something about it being bad luck, Josh seeing Meryl before the wedding. I couldn't help it. As far as I was concerned, at this point, they really needed some good luck on their side.

"It just doesn't seem wise," I whispered. "To take any risks. You know what I'm saying?"

"I hear you," Josh said, wiping at his face with the back of his hand. "But I don't think Meryl's big on bad luck right now. She wanted me to walk her down there. I'm just doing what I'm told."

I handed him her orchid, making sure he took it tightly, from the middle, so it didn't sag. "She's all yours," I said, already moving out of the suite to give them some time alone.

But then, as if on cue, Meryl appeared in the living room doorway in full attire. I had helped her get ready, but I hadn't seen her completely ready. Her dress was beaded and mermaid-shaped, flipping out, in a circle, on the floor. She was wearing these long, sparkling earrings that fell down all the way to her shoulders, a soft lace veil falling loosely behind her ears.

She looked like an absolute dream. I could hear Josh breathing in, a sharp intake — his hand, with the orchid in it, moving instinctively to his stomach. And I wish — I really wish — that I could begin to describe what it was like seeing her being seen that way by him. It was like watching a memory.

"You look amazing," he said.

"Thank you," she said, looking right back at him.

I looked back and forth between them. They didn't take their eyes off each other, not even for a second. Eye to eye, unblinking.

It made me think of a story that I'd read about Quaker weddings: how if you looked at each other a certain way, for a certain period of time, you married yourselves. That *that* was the whole of it. The deal done and sealed. It was so intimate a moment — so intimate a thing to watch — I wished I could disappear instantaneously, leaving the two of them alone. It was also hard not to look.

But before I could make my exit — before Josh could move closer to Meryl or Meryl could move closer to him; before Josh even said hello to Meryl, really — there was a loud noise in this glamorous hotel room, the loudest of noises, almost like someone had dropped a two-ton brick right above us. Or two hundred of them.

Then — in the quickest succession — the lights started to flicker brightly, and then less brightly, and there was a loud *whoosh* and the water spurted out of the air conditioner and the dimmers stopped being dim and everything all around us went completely out and off.

And everything went black.

One of my very first nights in Narragansett, a storm came in off the water, and the entire town lost its power. I was sitting downstairs at the Bon Vue, a local oceanside bar that — with the exception of college Thursdays — was exclusively frequented by town natives: carpenters and fishermen and store owners, the people who lived nearby. When the lights went out, everyone got quiet for a second, one lone voice calling out, "Here we go again." Then the candles were pulled out, the battery-radio turned on high, and everyone went back to drinking. Not so in one of the most prestigious hotels in New York City. First came the screeching, almost in harmony, coming out of almost every guest room. Doors were opening and closing, opening again. It wasn't so much the loss of light, but the loss of cold air — the air-conditioning reserve already starting to soften, heat coming up and in from the outside.

From up in Suite 2401, there was no way to know exactly what was going on downstairs: people running through the lobby and out onto the street to see if the power outage was widespread or exclusive only to the Essex House. Someone would say it was definitely all of Central Park South, someone else arguing that the Plaza, down the block, was fine. Hotel staff were gathering candles and towels in preparation for the night, starting to empty out the refrigerators. Thirty-four pounds of fresh fish were put on ice and then thrown away. For good measure, one hotel guest fainted center lobby, announcing she had heat stroke. Then she asked for a better room.

Upstairs, where we were, people were walking outside onto the balconies, into the natural light, talking to each other. What had happened? Where was the power? The guy on the balcony next to us announced that he was a scientist, and he was certain this had something to do with "overexertion of the main air-conditioning mechanism" downstairs.

"That takes a scientist?" Meryl whispered to me, walking back inside.

She took the hotel freesia candles out of the bathroom, and we sat in a semicircle around them on the living room floor.

"Aren't you worried your dress is going to wrinkle?" I said. "Let me get you a towel to sit on."

She waved me off. "Don't worry about it. In a couple of minutes, this dress is going to be stuck to me like glue anyway." She started to smile at me, her eyes lighting up. "It's kind of amazing though, isn't it? My mother is literally going to have a nervous breakdown."

I started to tell her not to worry about it — not to worry about any of it — that they'd get the power back on before the ceremony. But on a Sunday afternoon, during a holiday weekend, I seriously doubted that was true.

"You're not upset, Mer?" Josh said.

"Not at all." She shook her head. "Are you? At least now this wedding is going to be memorable. Not just another hotel wedding with the same hotel band and hotel flowers. Everyone at *our* wedding will be too busy standing around all hot and miserable. We might actually get to have a good time watching them."

Josh smiled at her, as an answer. It was weird, though, the smile — I didn't know how to read it. It was like all of a sudden he was watching her, watching all of this, from a great distance. I tried to make him look at me, make eye contact, and remind him he needed to focus. But he wouldn't turn my way.

"You know what?" I said, standing up. "I'm going to try to head Bess off at the pass. Make sure everything's going okay down below."

"Things are definitely not okay down below," Meryl said. "You're better off up here with us until absolutely necessary."

"It's going to be a long walk down," Josh added.

"I'll be fine," I said. "You guys just hang out up here a little longer and try to stay cool. Who knows? Maybe they'll even have the elevators running by the time you have to go down." I figured it didn't hurt to be hopeful.

"I'm betting they won't," Josh said, not so hopeful.

I started heading to the door and then thought of something. "How are you going to get in touch with us down there?" I said. "If there's some type of problem or something?"

"Some type bigger than this?" Meryl said.

It was a good point.

"I'll tell you what, Emmy," Josh said. "If

there are any more problems, I'll just scream really loud."

"Good idea," I said before leaving them alone, closing the door behind me as I went.

It was a very unhappy thing trying to walk down twenty-four high flights of stairs in a pair of strappy three-and-a-half-inch heels. I could feel them becoming a part of my feet: nail hitting heel, heel hitting calf. Around floor eleven, I decided to try a different tack, and take on the rest of the walk barefoot, especially after I saw a group of very blond sorority sisters from the University of Texas–Austin doing the exact same thing: whipping off their pumps, flipping them four flights below.

"Go for it," one of them whispered to me, holding up her own sandals as evidence that I should. Her nails were bright pink — the exact same shade as the heels in her hand. I almost admired this. "It's totally allowed in these situations."

It was also apparently allowed to use the hotel blackout as an excuse to get rip-roaring drunk in the middle of the afternoon — not that I would normally be one to judge for making such a decision. I could have used a drink myself right about then, and maybe would have asked for one, except that one of the girls, the whisperer of shoe-advice, happened to drop and break her bottle of Amstel Light as I took my left shoe off and stepped, newly barefoot, right on top of it.

"Oh, my God!" she said. "You're bleeding."

"Yes," I said, moving down a few more steps and trying to remove the several small slivers of beer glass wedged into my big toe, down the entire length of my sole. "Glass will do that."

It felt like one of the sole pieces hadn't come out — or at least a sliver of a piece hadn't come out — my skin tightening around whatever was still caught inside. I stood up anyway, ready to hobble the rest of the way down alone, and try to figure out a way to warn Meryl and Josh not to step into the same thing.

"Can I help?" she said.

I shook my head. "You know what?" I said. "I think I'll take it from here by myself."

By the time I made it to the Grand Salon, the hotel was really starting to boil. The air on reserve had drowned in the massive space. I tried to search for my mother in the midst of the chaos. The hotel staff was weaving in and out of the several hundred folding chairs set up for the ceremony. They were holding tiny paper fans — the kind that little kids would carry around — putting one on each chair. The one I'd had when I was younger was bright pink, and as I remember, Josh used to make fun of me for trying to use it. "Don't you know that the energy you use to fan yourself makes you hotter than just doing nothing at all?"

He was going to *love* having those here.

"Emmy! Thank God!"

I looked over to see my mom running toward me. She was in such a state — so preoccupied and consumed — that even when she reached me, she didn't notice how I was standing on the ball of my foot. One blessing.

"Emmy," she said again. "The Moynihan-Richardses are smoking a doobie with Bess in the back room."

"Excuse me?"

She leaned in and whispered. "That's apparently what they call marijuana these days."

"We need to change the subject immediately," I said.

She just looked at me. "They're sending

people home in the lobby. They're just telling them not to get out of their cabs because in a half hour or so they're saying the temperature's going to be hovering around a hundred degrees in here. Dad's standing there telling them to come in anyway. That we'll make do. . . . It's something of a blackout battle."

"Has anyone thought about just doing this outside? Why don't we just go across the street to Central Park?"

"Things are worse out there," she said, shaking her head, already looking past me, looking around the room for what needed doing. "It's a hundred degrees, and the sun's coming down full steam. Not that I don't think they should go through with it, even under these conditions. Of course I think they should go through with it, if that's what they want to do. They're the people who matter most today. No one else."

I shook my head in total amazement.

"What?" she said.

"You just have this really incredible power to surprise me," I said. "At the moments when I need you to most."

She rolled her eyes. Then she rolled them again, just in case I missed it. "I appreciate that, love, but we don't have time to be all dramatic about it right now," she said.

"Just tell me what you need me to do," I said.

"Well, we're going to have the ceremony in here," my mom said, pointing toward the center of the ballroom. "And then just an abbreviated version of the cocktail hour with drinks and the unperishables. Is unperishables even a word?"

"I'm not sure."

"Can you find out? I keep using it, but your father's looking at me like he thinks I made it up."

"Did you?'

She looked at me seriously. "It's possible," she said.

I'd never known much about making things beautiful. There were girls who were built that way, probably the same girls who knew from birth how they wanted their own weddings to be, everything already in place — every dried flower and champagne flute, every pressed napkin. I, on the other hand, was another kind of girl. You could show us how to dry a flower, and we would be able to do it. You could get us to shine-swipe a champagne flute. Hell, we could even set a fantastic china-filled table, given

310

the proper guidance. But the whole time, we'd be giggling on the inside, deep-down believing that all of it was just an extended version of playing with Mommy's makeup, waiting for someone to come in and get us in trouble.

So when I explain that the ballroom was beautiful when we were done, I say it with a sense of surprise that I had anything to do it with it. I imagined my wedding, if it ever came around, would involve nothing more than a beach and a little barbecue, some very rich chocolate cake. But for those twenty minutes that we had to make the Essex House's mostly windowless ballroom blackout-friendly, I was Martha Stewart living. Granted, one with an injured foot less than daintily wrapped in a cloth napkin beneath my fancy shoe, but a Martha Stewart nonetheless.

When we were done, there were tall mahogany candles everywhere, huge clusters of them forming a semicircle in the entranceway. We'd brought in antique lanterns from the basement, placed them in front of the flower bouquets: everything dark and lit and backlit and floral. Browns and deep blues present in the candlelight, the windows open just enough for the heat-wind to start kicking in, a drop of breeze making its way from the river.

The only trouble we had was with the stained glass window directly behind the altar — the fiery, unmitigated sun threatening to burn right down on Josh and Meryl, making them sweat. My mother came up with the idea of covering the window with the black garbage bags, still holding the ice for the affair. Bag balanced on bag balanced on bag. It looked somewhere between a modernist sculpture and an unfinished wall. But it almost didn't look like a mistake.

More of the guests had been dissuaded by the hotel's promise of hundred-degree temperatures than had been inspired by my father's plea that they stick it out, but there were about thirty people there, filling up the first several rows.

We had filled up the first row ourselves: me sitting next to my dad, my mom on his other side. Then Berringer and Michael and Bess and the Moynihan-Richardses. All of us were sitting there, semicircled around the small vine-inspired altar. The judge was standing, in wait, at the center of the altar.

Josh and Meryl had decided a long time ago to take religion out of the ceremony — no glass breaking and circle walking, and also no family priest performing. The part that I didn't know was that they had also decided that they didn't want anyone standing up there with them. Together, they'd walk down the aisle and be under the awning. Together, they'd stand there. Now we were all just waiting for it. In balmy 90-degree weather.

My dad slid back around in the seat next to me. And when I say slid, I mean that literally. We were all sticking to our seats, our feet to the floor.

"Are you going to get up and look for them?" I said.

"No," he said, shaking his head. He wasn't really looking at me, which scared me. It was another thing Josh seemed to inherit from our dad: They only looked away when they didn't want you to see something.

"Don't you think someone should go and look for them, maybe?" I was whispering, careful so my mom wouldn't hear me.

He looked worried, his eyebrows meeting on top of his nose. "They'll come down when they're ready," he said.

"Then why are you making that face?"

"I have a bad feeling they're not going to be," he said.

But before I could ask him why he thought that was, the music started — the one lone cellist who had decided to stick this out started to play her rendition of Canon in D. Everyone stood up, myself included, trying to get a clear view of the betrothed in the half-dark: Meryl in her princess dress, Josh beside her, his hand on her elbow. If this were all we'd have to remember this day by, wouldn't it end up looking like this was the only way it was ever supposed to be? So maybe I was wrong to be questioning it still. What did I know about the way things came together? Maybe they had to come this close to falling apart first.

Only — before I could think about the rest of it, before I could think about everything I did know — they were there, right before me, right before all of us, walking down the last stretch of aisle, holding hands. It didn't seem like real handholding though. It seemed to be more in the manner of one leading the other. I just wasn't sure which one was which.

I took a quick peek at my parents, who were clasping each other's hands tightly, my father keeping his eyes down. Then I looked back toward Josh and Meryl. They were at the front now, facing the judge, both of them sweating from their walk down the stairs, thin parallel lines running down their backs, Meryl's hair sticking tight against her head.

Josh looked over at her, squeezed her hand harder, before he leaned in and said something to the judge.

"If you'll all take your seats," the judge said. We did as we were told, quickly, everyone keeping their gaze straight on the two of them.

This is when they turned around and faced us.

Josh tried to give everyone a smile. "We wanted to thank you all for coming," he said. "That's first."

"And waiting," Meryl added.

He nodded his agreement, clearing his throat. "But because of the blackout going on here right now, obviously this isn't the best circumstance to get married, and so we're not going to be doing that today."

He was so backward in how he said it that you could have missed it. If you weren't paying close attention, you might have still been waiting for the ceremony to start. I wondered if part of Meryl was waiting herself, her hand wrapped so tightly around the orchid, tighter than the one holding Josh's.

Josh kept his eyes on her though. And eventually she looked back at him — believing him. Believing that this would turn out okay. I think it gave him courage, because he kept going.

"Obviously, we've been together forever, and we love each other very much. This is just a little shift in plans I'm talking about now. Not a cancellation or anything like that. Just a postponement, really." He tried to laugh. "Until a day when we can actually see each other."

Which was exactly when the lights came back on.

It was just a flicker at first, a blink, but then the whole room lit up like a jammed highway, bright and unquestioning: chandelier light floodlighting the candlelight, wall lamps now bright and gauzy against lanterns, half-light becoming full light, the regular world back in colorful 3D.

And standing there, under the fiercest spotlight of all, was Josh. What the light revealed about Josh. Meryl must have been looking for it first, but then we all were, and there was no denying what was on his face — a look of total and utter despair.

"Meryl . . . ," he said.

But it was too late. The orchid fell out of her hand — almost in slow motion — the flower falling to the floor. "Postpone your-self," she said, as if that made any sense.

I put my face in my hands.

"Tell the truth, Josh," she said, still only looking at him. Her face right in his, moving in closer. "You keep talking about the lights and circumstance and every other half-truth you can think of, but you said you were going to get up here and tell our families the truth."

He didn't say anything at first. No one did. What was there for us to say, anyway? The newly shining lights almost made them seem on a stage, performing. It seemed like this wasn't happening in real life. I had been absolutely prepared for Josh and Meryl to fall apart now and not prepared at all, which was the only reason I could even be sure that it really was hap-pening.

Which might be why I looked up behind them. To that one stained-glass-window garbage-bag sculpture, the light still peeking in between the bags' creases. Which was when I noticed one of the bags covering the window — one of the bags on the bottom tier, water dripping into it, heat beaming onto it — wasn't exactly like the others. It was fatter, misshapen.

It had a bright blue drawstring tied in a

double knot on the top of it.

It was my bag.

My tapes. My tapes *cooking* inside! It was like I could envision them in there — curling into themselves, shriveling and cracking irrevocably. And I could envision the rest of it: how, in the chaos, they never made it up to my parents' hotel room. How my father must have taken them out of the car, intending to take them to the cool suite, but he was needed for something, he got sidetracked and dropped them here. And then, for all the wrong reasons, someone placed them in the window with the other garbage bags, a sacrifice, to take in all of the heat, all of the day's relentlessly boiling sun.

"Oh, my God!"

The words came out of me in a primal way, in a voice I didn't really even recognize as my own, until I saw everyone turning toward me, shocked. Josh included. He, of course, thought I was responding to what was happening to him. How could he know anything else? How could anyone begin to imagine it would be happening twice, at once, both of us losing everything we had been holding on to so tightly? The two of us losing exactly what we had been most afraid to lose, that thing we kept plugging ahead with, the main excuse we'd used again and again, to not let ourselves change in the ways we needed to most.

Josh's and my eyes met, and I could see it. He wanted me to say something. He wanted me to say something else to break the silence. He wanted me to say something else to save him.

And when I didn't, he started to. But before he could, there was movement all around. Dr. Moynihan-Richards stood up to his full five-foot height, ready and eager to come to his daughter's aid. Watching him, Michael stood up also. Then Bess, straightening her dress as she went. All of them were ready to pounce if they needed to — this family who was just about to join ours, now permanently against it. Which was when we all stood up also: Berringer first, ready to help Josh, my father. My mother. When I stayed seated at first, my eyes still garbage-bag-bound — drawn tunnel-like to the blue string — my mother reached across my father and pulled me up by the shoulder until I was at full height too.

I took one last look at my bag of tapes, crushed into the window, and then focused on the issue more presently at hand. Ready to conquer Mrs. Moynihan-Richards if the situation called for it.

I could take her.

But this — this next part — this is what I try to hold on to most. For a moment, Josh stopped looking at Meryl, and turned instead to look out at all the rest of us, everyone in the first row, and everyone behind us, if not in apology then in announcement of what I already knew. If someone were to blame here, it was him. He knew it better than anyone. He understood it.

And in his acknowledgment, I stopped needing to. To blame him, that is. Everyone else would make sure to do plenty of that. I was going to need to do something else. Meanwhile, outside, the hotel-world was starting to come back: the hum of the resurrected air conditioner and a hundred appliances that must have been left plugged in before the chaos — blow-dryers and printers, one loud stereo. In trying to stay cool, we hadn't closed the door to the ballroom, so we heard all of it. The phones ringing and elevators running, and right outside in the ballroom foyer, a girl screaming to her friend or her family or someone else she thought she knew, still a little too far out of her reach — who had taken something from her that she was trying, desperately, to get back. In just one more minute, she'd realize she couldn't.

And my brother said, "I can't do this."

part five

This is how it ends?
Of course not. No.
This is how it begins.
— Sadie Everett

Well.

Where do we go from here? I started off this crazy weekend by trying to make sense of these moments — these moments that you know you're going to remember — but like anything else, nothing exists without its opposite. So maybe it makes a certain kind of sense that I ended up thinking about the moments you know you'll forget. Or, more accurately, try to remember incorrectly. How do we all learn how to do that? Relive something again and again in our heads until it takes on a slightly different light, a less truthful tone, until the memory can't injure us as directly, until it joins the ranks of the more manageable?

When I look back to that moment when Josh finally spoke — silencing everything else — I think: Maybe this is what storytelling is made for. So someone can sit up front and raise their hand, showing off with an answer. Saying: This may have been uncomfortable, it may be uncomfortable for right now, but soon it will be over. Soon, I will explain the part to you where we all get to go home.

Let me tell you this. One of the strangest things to happen after the wedding that didn't — after everyone started leaving the ballroom in droves, Josh and Meryl first, the back-rowers following — was that one guest told another how much she liked her dress. They were just standing in the aisle, and I didn't recognize either of them. But this I remember most vividly, the holding on to the green fabric, the eye-to-eye contact of the exchange, their separation from each other. Like this was the most important thing that happened, or at least what they'd take away. The idea both stunned and comforted me.

As for me, I wasn't sure which way to go. I had my tapes with me, in my hand. Walking up to the stained-glass window had been like approaching a locked apartment. You knew it was useless. You knew it. But you turned the knob anyway. A quick peek in the bag revealed the rest. For the most part, the tapes were gnarled and warm and ruined.

I looked around the still-panicked lobby

and tried to find a place for myself. I wasn't going back to the bridal suite for anything in the world. I could just picture the scene up there: Josh and Meryl taking the stairs to get there and then remembering halfway up that the elevator was working again. So maybe they'd get out of the staircase on floor seven or floor nine and ride the rest of the way. And once they were inside, they would do it again, exactly what they'd just done in front of everyone — tell each other it was over, end things — so they'd get to believe it.

Bess was on a courtesy phone in the lobby's corner. I had no idea whom she was calling, but Michael was with her, the Moynihan-Richardses a few feet behind. In the corner was my father, saying good-bye to people, trying to talk them down from whatever it was they thought they'd just seen.

The whole hotel world was still moving in fast-forward: the bellhops and elevators, the now-useless towel piles. I decided to go outside and get some air. I wanted to give everything a little time to calm down. Or forever to calm down. But just as I was heading through the revolving door out onto the street, I heard someone knocking hard on the glass from the partition behind. It was my mother, motioning for me, frantically, to revolve the door right back in.

She looked down at the bag in my hand as we stepped back onto the lobby floor, but didn't say anything. I don't know if she hadn't made the connection yet that the tapes were ruined, or if she just didn't want to make it yet.

"I need you to take the Moynihan-Richardses back to the house," she said. "You need to go there right now with them because they want to drive home tonight. All the way to Arkansas. As soon as possible."

Her voice was all business, not that I would have argued anyway. I was glad for any excuse to get out. Even this one.

"And listen, Emmy, okay? I'm not sure if anyone else is actually planning on staying with us at this point, but if I'm the one who tries to make them go, they'll end up staying for three days. I'll make them all dinner. I'll invite them to stay on for the rest of the week."

"I'll take care of it, Mom," I said. "I promise."

"Because I need the house empty, Em. By the time I get back there tonight, I want everyone gone except for the four of us. We need to be there alone for a while, don't you think?" She paused, looking up at the ceiling as far away from the bottom of me as she could get. "And please. Soak your foot for a good half hour when you can, okay?"

I looked down at the napkin, peeking out from beneath my heel, revealing my own little injury. In all of the chaos, I'd almost forgotten.

"Just sit there and soak it," she continued. "Put about a half-tablespoon of salt in the water."

"I'll put lots of salt in it," I said. "What else do you need me to do for you?"

She shook her head, her hand tugging gently on the bottom of my hair, flipping it under. "Nothing."

"Then where are you going to be?" I said.

"I'm going to be with your father," she said. "Wherever he decides to take me."

It didn't used to be that the time right after people got married was designated for the betrothed taking a major trip together. The whole trip-taking situation grew out of a much simpler tradition in Northern Europe of drinking a certain kind of mead and honey wine post-ceremony that was supposed to bring good luck. You were supposed to keep drinking it for a month — or a moon — which was where the term *honeymoon* came from. After this wedding, though, I was certain that the only wine drinking taking place was happening in the Volvo I was driving with the Moynihan-Richardses: the two of them sitting in the back together — chauffeur-style, on either side of the car seat, either side of a buckled-in Papa Smurf — both of them taking hefty swigs from the jug they'd lifted from somewhere inside the hotel.

Dr. Moynihan-Richards kept offering me some, in an attempt, I think, to let me know he didn't blame me for what happened back in the ballroom. For the mess this weekend had become.

"We blame your brother, not you," he came right out and said at one point. "And your parents. But them only a little bit."

I smiled at him in the rearview. "Thank you," I said.

It didn't seem like the appropriate time to point out that he could have been justified in blaming me too. Especially because I had pretended to be their daughter's friend when, clearly, being a true friend to her hadn't turned out to be what mattered most to me. I thought about what was going on with her back at the hotel. With both of them. Who was where now? How was anyone trying to help each other? I had this image of the two of them sitting in opposite corners of the living room in that huge suite, talking to each other in starts and stops — both of them wanting to leave, but knowing they couldn't. Knowing that when they did, that would be it.

I flipped on the radio, searching for an AM station not playing a commercial. "How about we listen to a traffic report? See what the highways are going to be like for your trip home?"

But Mrs. Moynihan-Richards leaned forward over the front seat, flipping the radio back off and wrapping her fingers around my seat's edges.

"We're going either way," she said. "What's the difference what they tell us about it?"

"I guess that's one way to look at it," I said, not excited about having Mrs. M-R right in my personal space. This was the first time I was even having anything approaching a real conversation with her. It was also, considering the extreme circumstances of today, probably going to be the last.

And still, I just wanted her to sit back,

something she seemed determined not to do.

"So here's a question for you," she said, staying where she was. "Were those your videos I saw you put in the back? Videos of the documentary Meryl has told us you've been working on in Rhode Island? About fishermen?"

"About their wives," I corrected. "Yes, those were my tapes," I said. Because they were my tapes. They *were,* in the absolutely painful past tense of the word. I imagined I could salvage a few of them — but there was very little I could do to get most of them back, most of the stories that would die with them. Still, it was possible some of the tapes could be saved. It was possible that this wasn't over yet.

"I don't know much about videos, but they looked kind of . . . troubled," Dr. Moynihan-Richards said.

Thanks, genius, I wanted to say. But I ignored him, or I tried to. He was leaning forward now too, his arms locked around the empty passenger seat.

Mrs. M-R shot him a look. "Meryl was saying you try to make movies that end well? That that's your overall movie-making goal?"

I nodded, even though it made me

cringe a little to hear someone say it out loud. It just sounded so hokey, and also it reminded me how far I'd been from finding this film's ending, how I had been just about equally far from one with my endless tapes of footage as I was now that my footage was ruined.

He caught my eye in the rearview, squinting at me, apparently entirely unsatisfied with my nod-as-response answer. "But don't you think that's a bit of a sad enterprise?" he said. "Trying to make movies in that way?"

"Which way?" I asked him.

"Happy," he said.

"Well, not to be the bearer of bad news here," Mrs. Moynihan-Richards said, "but I think we're missing the larger issue, which is why you'd choose to put your footage in a garbage bag in the first place. On the subconscious level, at least, there is no question that disposal had to be your main intention. The placement of the tapes in the garbage bag alone makes that much clear."

Dr. Moynihan-Richards nodded at his wife in agreement. I had forgotten for a minute that they were sociology professors, but I remembered it again in how they were looking at each other, how they were looking at me, like a case study. A case study of a girl who put everything she thought mattered most right into the garbage. The only problem with their theory was that, in my experience, my subconscious worked in trickier ways. Considering how I'd been living the last few years, I thought I could make a fairly compelling argument that if I were really trying to get rid of the tapes, a garbage bag would be the last place I'd put them.

Dr. M-R leaned closer to me. "So did you really think that you'd finish the film eventually? That you'd find the ending you were looking for?"

I turned my eyes back to the road. "I think I was hoping something else would happen."

"Which was what?"

I looked right at them. "That someone would tell me," I said.

"Tell you what?" Mrs. M-R said.

"What to do next," I said.

She looked at me for another second before sitting back again, holding her wine jug closer to herself, looking back out the window. Dr. M-R followed suit.

"Well," she said. "That's even sadder."

Then she was quiet. So was he. But I could still feel them sneaking looks at me, even when they thought I couldn't any-more: not mean looks, but looks of pity, which were worse as far as I was con-cerned. I could feel their looks, and I could feel my heart beating, and the tapes — in the back — I swear: I could feel them weighing the wagon completely down.

And before I could think about it any-more — because I really couldn't think about it anymore — I pulled the car off the highway, onto the shoulder, and halted the ignition. And with the Moynihan-Richardses of the Ozark Mountains as my only witnesses, I took the bag of tapes out of the back and threw it. I threw it as far as my hands and injured foot would let me — as far as I could throw it away from me. They almost looked like seagulls, the tapes did, flying out of the top of the bag into the distance. Sick seagulls, more like, dying seagulls. Because they landed in the grass, no more than ten feet from where they started.

I wouldn't say I was happy looking out at them — the defeated remains of the last three years of my life — but I did have a feeling of relief. I was deeply relieved that, if nothing else, I wasn't dying out there with them.

I got back in the station wagon and,

without a word, turned on the ignition and headed back out onto the highway, back in the direction of home. It was only when we were moving again that Mrs. Moynihan-Richards spoke.

She kept her voice down low. "Can I go ahead and assume that you have other copies?"

"Only," I said, "if you want to assume wrong."

I don't remember all that clearly saying good-bye to the Moynihan-Richardses, and getting myself into the house. Getting the M-Rs into their RV, getting them gone. When I was inside, though, the entire place was empty, and incredibly quiet. Almost eerily so. I still wasn't quite sure what to take from that car ride with them yet, how to digest exactly what I'd left on the roadside. I didn't feel any relief that the tapes were gone from me now — that my never-ending project had found an ending. I didn't feel a great sadness either though. If I had to name it, what I did feel was a space opening up inside me — a larger space than I could remember being there in a long time. I felt longing.

I went into the kitchen and wrote a quick note on my mom's panda-bear pad and taped it to the front door.

This is what it said: "Go away now. Thanks!"

Then I headed up to my room, slowly. I didn't turn any lights on as I felt my way toward the familiar staircase, crawling up the stairs to my bedroom, and opened the door half-expecting to find anything except what I found.

Berringer.

He was lying there, just lying on my bed, like it was his right. On top of the blanket. Fully dressed, except for his shoes. I was going to ask him how he got back here before me, but I didn't really care. I didn't really care how he got here, or what exactly had happened first. It didn't seem to matter so much.

Instead, I sat on the edge of my bed and didn't say anything for a while. I didn't move at all. Neither did he. He kept his hand on my back though, the entire time I sat there, his fingers pressing in softly. My heart was beating so fast, I was worried he could feel it through his fingertips. I was worried that this was why he was keeping his hands there: to steady me.

Eventually, I took off my shoes and put them right by Berringer's, and I took down my hair. Then I stood up again and locked the door. I lay down next to him. Berringer watched me do all of this, not saying a word. At least I think he was watching me.

In the dark, I could see him blinking. My whole left side was touching his whole right side — side arm to side arm, hip to hip, side leg to side leg. Foot to bad foot.

"You hurting?" he said.

"I've been better."

He didn't say anything. But he turned toward me, leaning on his elbow, waiting for me to continue.

"I made things worse today," I said.

He shook his head. "You don't have that much power."

I kept lying there on my back, but I turned my head to face him too. I started to ask why Celia hadn't been at the wedding earlier. But then I realized I didn't have to, not right then. Even if I didn't know why yet — if he hadn't actually said out loud that after the rehearsal dinner they'd had a discussion, that he told her he didn't think he could see her anymore — I knew that it was over with her. I just knew it. Berringer didn't work any other way. It was nice, among these boys whom I loved, that someone didn't.

Berringer turned me on my side away from him and started unzipping my dress. His hands were cold and quick on my bare skin, like glass.

"Let's just rest for a while," he said. His

hands were on my stomach now, criss-crossed around each other, holding me.

"With your hands like that?" I said.

"We could try," he said.

I turned around to face him, his hands on my back. "Okay," I said, but I was already kissing him while I said it. He looked so nervous that it freed me somehow to not feel it myself — how nervous I was.

Which was a good thing.

Because if I had done anything differently — if I had looked away from him, had let him look away from me, if he hadn't touched my skin, lying down above me, close, we might have thought better of this.

We might have stopped.

But instead he held me there, pushing my hair back with his fingers, his eyes open on my eyes, watching, everything happening so slowly at first, as though we'd been here, right here, a thousand times instead of one, as though this time we might be able to hold on to it. Locate it. Something old and quiet and lost that you can see again for just a few seconds, see in a bright flash, before you have to blink, close your eyes against it, start to quickly let go.

I must have drifted off because when I woke up, I was naked and Berringer was gone, which made me *feel* more naked. I got up slowly, but I felt it anyway — the sharp squeeze of it — my heartbeat moving around in my foot. I lay back down, taking an uncomfortable breath in. As I did, my cell phone started ringing from the bed. I reached for it, careful not to move my foot, which was as heavy as a cannon.

JOSH.

Man. "Where are you?" I said.

"The city still," he said. "Where are you?"

"Home."

"You're home?"

I cleared my throat. I didn't know what else to say. I didn't want to bring up Meryl, or push him on what was happening with her back at the hotel. I wanted him to tell me when he was ready. I was hoping, now, he wouldn't have any trouble actually telling me when he was ready.

"Listen," he said. "I'm actually looking for Berringer. Did he come by the house? Have you seen him anywhere?"

I shot up, grabbing for my dress. "Why would I have I seen him anywhere? Why would I have seen Berringer? Anywhere?" I knew I was rambling, but I couldn't help it.

"Emmy," he said. "Easy."

"I'm easy," I said. Again, not really the best response.

"Look, if he calls the house, will you just tell him I'm looking for him? I was supposed to meet him at midnight. But I'm going to be a little late."

Midnight. I was supposed to meet Matt at midnight. I turned and looked at the clock: 11:36. Oh, my God. It was 11:36. The diner was fifteen minutes away. If I got up right now and didn't even shower — if I put on the first thing I saw — I might be able to be there on time.

"Hey, Josh, I really have to go," I said. "I'll see you when you get back here okay?"

But he didn't hear me.

"What?" he said.

There was no time to repeat.

So I just hung up.

There were a couple of rules of the universe that I had learned, and felt like I could stand by. The first was that if I was in a rush to get anywhere — whether it was to get married or get to where I was going or to find out what happened next in my life — I would inevitably be late for it, slow myself down, as soon as I dared say the words out loud, as soon as I admitted, even in my head, that I wanted to be somewhere else, right then.

The second was that my mother would make me eat something first.

I opened the front door, holding the car keys, to find her and my dad on the other side of it, no longer in their wedding clothes — my dad carrying the tallest white box I'd ever seen.

"When did you get home?" he said from behind it.

"When did you guys get home?" I said.

I started shaking out my bad foot, holding on to the doorknob for support. My mom instinctively looked down at it, her eyes moving up and checking out my outfit: sky pajama pants with very sparkly clouds all over them, and a white V-neck T-shirt that said "I ♥ Mt. Airy Lodge" across the chest in matching sky blue.

"That's a great look for you," she said, nodding at my outfit before motioning for me to get out of the way so my dad could get into the house. She followed behind him. "Come into the kitchen with me for a minute. I want to talk to you."

"Mom, I'm really late," I said, pointing to the front door with the scribbled note still on it.

She was already in the kitchen. "Well, you're going to have to be a little later then," she called back to me.

I crumpled the note up, following her into the kitchen, reluctantly, and taking a seat on one of the stools. My dad was putting the box on the counter. He removed the top, slowly, revealing the glorious yellow pineapple cake. All six tiers of it.

"It's bad luck not to eat some of the wedding cake," my mom said, taking a seat on the stool across from me, pushing her hair back off her face.

"But they didn't get married," I said.

She gave me a look. "Are you going to argue with me about everything for my entire life? Let me know now."

My dad kissed us both on the forehead — my mom first, then me — before heading toward the stairs. "You can bring mine up to me," he said. "I need to take a shower for the next nine hours."

"I'll meet you in there," my mom said, watching him go. And, just like when I was little and lived here, I had the same strange reaction I always had when I watched them flirt: somewhere between nausea and relief. She turned back to me, smiling. "Now," she said, taking two forks out of the container on the counter, handing one to me. "I want to hear exactly what you're thinking."

"About what, Mom?

"Where your brother's going now. After he deals with tonight, obviously, and this mess he's made. Which is quite a mess, I might add." She closed her eyes, as if against the whole situation. "Do you think that he is going to see her now? To his other friend?"

"You know about his other friend?" I said. "You know about Elizabeth?"

"Is that her name?" She held her bite of cake in front of her mouth. "That's a nice name," she said.

"That seems to be the consensus."

She put the bite of cake in her mouth, starting to chew slowly. "Eat just a little," she said.

I shook my head, looking at the bottom tier — the sugary-white inside showing from where my mom had taken her scoop. "I can't," I said. "I told you. I'm really running late."

She looked at me questioningly as if to say, For what? I didn't answer, which, I guess, was the only answer she needed.

"Ahh," she said, putting her fork down.

"Mom, I'm not . . . I'm not getting re-started with that. With Matt, I mean. I love him. But I can't. I know that now. I do know that," I said.

And as soon as the words were out, I knew that I was telling her the truth. I understood, finally, that I couldn't go back to Matt, and not worry, every day, about ending up right back here again. In this place where I had no idea how to really begin to make myself happy.

"You know, I've got to say, I'm not sure I understand my children," she said, wiping her hands on her napkin. She pointed toward the front door. "That one spends years moving between two women, hoping one of them will eventually make the decision for him that only he can make. And this one organizes her life so even the choices she makes, she is always making the other one at the same time. She leaves, she stays. She stays exactly where she leaves."

I tried to smile at her, which made me start to tear.

"When you were little, you were always saying that Josh got to make all the choices because he was older. 'Why does he get to make all the decisions around here, Mom?' you'd say. 'How is that fair?' So for your seventh birthday, your father said you could pick where we went on the summer trip. You could pick any city in America as far away as Seattle, as close as Manhattan. You know which city you picked?"

I knew it without her even saying that much. I'd always known it, and I was starting to understand something else too — where she was going with this. What I wouldn't allow myself to see before now.

"London," I said.

"London," she repeated. "And the thing was, it didn't matter how many times I told you that we weren't paying for four plane tickets to London. That a driving trip was the only option. It was like you couldn't see anything else. And when even Dad took out that map and tried to explain to you that London wasn't even in America, you just kept arguing with him. 'But I want to go to London. It's the best city in America. I'll only go there.' For weeks around here. You were like a broken record."

"Where did we end up going instead that year?" I said, trying to remember. I couldn't recall it.

"Hershey, Pennsylvania . . . which you loved. You turned to your father the very first day there and said, 'Dad, I think Hershey, Pennsylvania, is even better than London would have been.'"

Hershey. All I could visualize with any certainty was the car ride up there, sitting behind my father in the backseat, staring sullenly at the back of his head. "Really? I said that?"

"No." She shook her head. "You complained the entire time. 'This restaurant isn't London. This candy store isn't London. Over here, this isn't London either.'"

"How can I not remember?"

She shrugged, picking up her fork again,

fixing a bite for me this time. "You were too busy complaining."

I took the bite from her. It was sweet and fruity and a little on the warm side — from the car or the blackout or both. The taste stayed strong in my throat. "I'm sorry about that," I said.

"You don't have to be sorry," she said. "You just have to try to understand what I'm telling you. I've told you the story of how your dad and I met, right?"

"Only a couple dozen times."

"But do you remember?"

"Of course I remember," I said. "You saw him and you left the bathroom and you knew you had to be with him. You just knew. From that moment on. It would be the two of you."

"Absolutely not," she said.

I looked at her in disbelief. "Okay," I said. "You're really starting to freak me out here."

"What I knew was that if I walked out of the bathroom and said good-bye to him, I would be fine. I would go to the play and meet someone else — if not that afternoon, then another afternoon — and I'd have an entirely different life. I'd be married to this new person or I wouldn't. Or I'd rekindle my romance with my first boyfriend,

Neiman Mortimar, who happens to be the biggest distributor of women's prom dresses anywhere in the Northeast, now. And I'd have a different house. Different furniture. White furniture, maybe. And I'd have these big, wonderful Shabbat dinners. And I'd like my mother-in-law very, very much."

"Susan Mortimar? The tiny woman with the cane at Whole Foods who you always say hi to? The one with the pink hair, and the mini-size cart?"

"Isn't she lovely?"

I couldn't help it anymore. I really started to cry. Pineapple was sticking the wrong way in my throat. My mother moved in closer to me, covering the space of the counter between us.

But she didn't reach for my hand, or lean farther forward so she could touch my face. She just shrugged. "What happened the day I met your father," she said, "is that I learned you have to choose. For better or for worse. You have to choose what your life is going to look like."

I tried to swallow, tried to think of what I wanted to say, what I was really thinking. "I just don't feel like I have good choices yet," I said. "It makes it hard to give up the old ones."

She waved me off. "Well. You're behind all that anyway," she said. "You're still stuck on the same part you were stuck on at seven."

"What part is that?"

"The part where you need to choose among the choices that are there, and not the ones that aren't anymore. At least not how you need them to be. You're still stuck on some imaginary idea you have of how it could have been. You need to think about how it is now. And how you want it to be."

How it might have been. How I want it to be. The list was forming in my head. In the "might have been" column there was Matt and me, Meryl and Josh. There was a trip to London that still hadn't happened, and there was a future — a hundred of them, or one — that I still hadn't begun to imagine. What was in the "how I want it to be" column? What could I find to put there? Did a new set of questions count?

But I didn't ask her. I didn't say anything. Not when what I was thinking was, I had no idea how far my life had gotten from any life I had wanted for myself. I was living in a small town, all alone, which would have been fine if I had chosen it for myself. But I had just *not* chosen anything else, and all of a sudden, it became very clear to me that this wasn't at all the same thing.

My mom took her fork back, making herself a final bite, big and full of icing. "And don't be offended, okay? But I wouldn't wear that shirt again. No one *really* loves the Mt. Airy Lodge. Even when they pretend to."

I was just under twenty minutes late by the time I got to the diner. It didn't look like it had changed a drop in the last decade: big open windows lining the entire restaurant, large white pillars on either side of the entranceway, a huge neon sign shining in bright pink. I searched for a spot, parking the car haphazardly near the garbage tub in the back, making a beeline on my one good foot for the front door. All of a sudden I couldn't get there fast enough.

It wasn't that I was looking forward to saying no to Matt, or that I had magically figured out what I needed to say in order to completely let him go. But I did want to tell him I was sorry for leaving the motel room — not because it was the wrong thing to do, but because I finally understood that it stopped us from doing the only right thing. Saying good-bye in a way that I would believe it was for real. I was ready to do that now. And I wanted, very badly, to wish him luck in Paris. I wanted to wish him luck.

Only, when I got to the diner, he was already gone. The host told me he came in earlier and didn't even sit down. He didn't sit down or even really take a look around. He just handed him a large manila envelope and asked him to give it to a girl named Emmy.

"And I take it you're the girl named Emmy?" he said, pronouncing it "E-my" in a thick Greek accent. "I take it you're not going to order anything either. You know this isn't a messenger service."

"I'm sorry," I said, taking the envelope from him. "I really appreciate it."

I tried to smile at him, which he wasn't having any of, and went outside to the front steps. I took a seat by the banister and opened the envelope, slowly, afraid to see what he'd written to me.

But inside there was no letter for me. There was no real note — no card even.

There was just a little arrow drawn on the envelope's flap pointing downward, THIS STILL BELONGS TO YOU written in all caps right above the arrow's stem.

I opened the envelope wider.

And, there, tucked into the deep left

corner, something glistened back at me. My engagement ring.

I reached in, carefully taking it out, holding it in my hand. This part of Matt and me — this tangible part of what our life had been together. I flipped the ring onto my pinky finger, holding it to my mouth. And then there I was: back in a motel room in Narragansett. I was looking up at the ceiling. I was taking the ring off my finger. I was about to do what I had to do one last time. I was saying good-bye.

It was a tricky kind of luck, saying it to myself because I, alone, was left to believe it. But this time, it felt like Matt was saying it too. From just beyond the parking lot, where he had driven away sometime before I arrived. When had he decided that was the thing to do? This morning when he woke up, thinking about us, or — maybe — on the way over here, thinking, again. Maybe when didn't matter. It just mattered that he came to the same decision. And for the first time, in a very long time, both of us were giving the other exactly what we needed.

Matt had left the ring in Scarsdale this whole time because he hadn't wanted to look at it either. He hadn't wanted to look at it any more than I had, which maybe wasn't the worst way for both of us to remember that it counted. But that it wasn't going to count for everything. Knowing that, the distance between us started to disappear. And I had the smallest trickle of what was to come — a glimpse of the truth of this whole thing — which was that the distance between us would come, and it would go. It would be different, and it wouldn't be so different. I'd remember Matt, and I'd remember him wrong. And that was probably when I'd miss him most.

From behind me, I heard knocking and turned around to see the host with his nose pressed up to the diner's glass front door, flattened there against it, his hands on either side.

"You okay?" he mouthed to me through the pane.

I smiled at him.

"Almost," I mouthed back.

"Well," he said, opening the door. "Then can you almost get off of my steps?"

I had one more stop to make.

My plan, initially, was to go right back to the house and meet Josh — call him if he wasn't back yet — but along the way, I couldn't do that. I wasn't even sure I remembered how to find my way to this place, exactly, especially in the dark. There were so few times I'd been there, and all of them had been so long ago.

But the thing was, I was going to figure it out, right then, even if it was the last thing I did.

Berringer was playing basketball in the driveway when I pulled up. He was standing right under the hoop and throwing one *swish* in after the other, catching the ball as it came through the net. The driveway was dark, so he was playing under the beam of his car's headlights. He looked soft, flushed, in the glow.

I walked up to him slowly. "Aren't you

afraid you're going to wake the neighbors?" I said.

He looked over at me, fairly surprised, holding the ball under his arm and smiling.

"Air ball," he said. "Safe at any hour of the night."

I smiled back. He was standing so close, I could feel heat coming from his legs. I worried he could feel my heart beating. Even if he couldn't, I could tell he was looking to me for clues as to what to do. I didn't want to stand there and make him feel like he had to say anything to me, but I couldn't make myself leave either.

"You missed him by about six minutes," he said, switching the ball over to the other arm. "He just left."

"Josh?"

He nodded. "He said he was going to head over to the pool."

"The Scarsdale pool? Why?" I put my hand up. "You know what? I take the question back. I don't want to know."

"I won't tell you then. I won't even give you a hint." He paused, and I could tell he was having trouble figuring out what he was trying to say. "But you should know, about earlier, I mean about us . . . I was stuck in the bathroom. I didn't just disappear on you. I wouldn't do that."

I shook my head. "You don't have to explain."

"No, I know. But I was. Stuck there. I heard your mom rummaging around in the linen closet and I didn't have my pants on and I didn't know how to go out there without causing alarm. For a minute I thought she was opening the bathroom door, and I jumped into the shower."

I felt myself starting to smile. "You could have actually been in the shower, you know. You could have actually been sleeping there, even," I said. "You are Josh's best friend."

"See? Where were you with that kind of guidance when I needed it? This is what they call a day late and a dollar short."

I started laughing, so did he.

But then we stopped.

"The thing I'm thinking, Emmy, is maybe we should talk about this," he said. "About what happened. If you want to talk about it."

I started to say I did, but really I wasn't sure I could. If he was just going to say something to try to make me feel okay about it — make me feel okay about us going our separate ways — I'd rather just leave the whole thing where it was. In a place where, for a few moments, I felt really happy again.

"What's there to talk about?" I said. "Isn't this just the part when you save my life?"

He smiled at me — a big, round smile. And for a second, I thought that was what he was going to say he wanted to do. As if he could. As if anyone could do that for me now but me.

"What if I said that you always have a place to stay in San Francisco? If you ever need one?"

"I'd say that sounds great," I said. Then I squeezed his hand, squeezed it like I meant it, and started to walk away. But he reached for my arm, holding on. He really held me there.

"You know," he said. "You could plan to need a place to stay. We could make a plan for that sort of thing. People do that."

"Which people?" I said.

"Just some people I know," he said. "People who can actually, you know, admit they like someone a little."

"Ha, ha," I said, looking down. I was blushing, my face getting redder by the second. And I knew that even in the dark, he knew that I was blushing. And he knew I couldn't stop.

He flipped the ball into the air, caught it. "You don't have to say it now or anything," he said. "Just one day."

"One day," I said, looking at him again. "But before I start planning any trips, I definitely have to go back to Rhode Island for a little while and quit my job and get my stuff and move it somewhere."

"Back here?"

"No, I can't make my mother that happy," I said. "It would be bad for the team. I'm thinking Los Angeles. Film school, maybe, or just getting a job somehow more related to film than fish."

"But no more Narragansett?"

"No more," I said. And it sounded right. It sounded so right, I couldn't deny it. The documentary was over. I wasn't going to start it again, even though, in theory, I could. I could try to get it right this time. But really, I had no idea how, and I knew I couldn't spend any more time trying to figure it out: how to *really* start again, or to steer it toward where I thought it needed to go. I understood, now, that I could say the same thing — the exact same thing — about Matt.

"I just don't think that I really have anything to go back to there," I said.

He nodded. "That sounds like a good

reason to try something else."

It did. To me too.

"You know, they have a great program at Stanford. I mean I don't know that much about these things, but I hear it's *arguably* the best documentary film program in the country. I'm not saying that for me," he added quickly. "I'm just saying."

I smiled at him. "Well, I appreciate you . . . saying."

We were both quiet. I wanted him to say something else. Anything else. That was all I wanted.

But maybe it was my turn. "Why don't I call you when I get out there?" I said. "Maybe you could come and visit."

"Or we could meet in the middle," he said. "And I'm not trying to be all symbolic. Big Sur is in the middle, and Monterey. It's incredible there. And there's this great restaurant right on the water near Carmel. It's in this old cabin. Tiny place, like six tables total. A buddy of mine is the chef there. He's an incredible chef, actually. Not as incredible as me, but, you know . . ." He smiled. "I may even have to have an actual meal."

"Then I'm in," I said, and I was. It was incredible there — that whole area along the California coast. I had been there as a little girl, and I liked the idea of going back. I liked the idea of all of it, really: the idea of driving up the coast, and having something I was excited about checking out, someone I was excited to see. And maybe something I was excited about getting back to also.

"So then I'll call you, I guess, " I said. "You're in my phone." I held it up for him to see.

"I'm in your phone," he said.

I looked down, feeling shy all over again. If this were the right thing to be doing, shouldn't I not have felt so shy? Shouldn't it just have felt familiar already? Easy? I wasn't sure. I wasn't sure this wasn't in fact the beginning of the very best part. And still, back at the house people would be swarming around — my mom, my father, Josh eventually. There would be a lot of explaining to do, a lot of time to feel out what would happen next. It would, in the end, be a little while before I could make that call to Berringer. But before I left him now, I took a long look at his face to remind myself that I wanted to make it. I really did want to.

Berringer reached out and touched my ear, pulling my hair behind it gently. "You've got such a nice face," he said.

I smiled. I smiled, and then looked down, mostly because I was just about to tell him the same thing.

Which seemed like a good place to start.

When I began thinking about Josh's wedding toast — when I began doing all the research about different wedding customs for it — I stumbled on all this information about the history of toasts itself. It turns out that there was an ancient French custom of putting a scorched piece of bread in the bottom of wineglasses — back when wine still needed to be decanted because of all the heavy sediments. The toast would absorb all that residue. It would absorb what was misplaced so you could enjoy what it was you were meant to enjoy. The French called this process "toasted." That was where the word came from.

And while I was driving all over my hometown late in the night after the wedding that never happened, after the fireworks and the bachelor party and the road trip and the blackout, and my mother's wet-naps and the pineapple cake and the broken blinker — that small broken directional arrow — and the lost love and the unlived lives, I thought about what I would say in a toast to my brother, at this point, if he ever needed me to make one again. And for the first time, in a long while, I had the answer to something. I knew the answer unequivocally.

I'd find my way here — I'd start with what happened here — the Scarsdale Pool. For the second time in the longest and shortest weekend of my life.

When I got there, I saw Josh's lone car in the parking lot under the three lit parking lot lamps, light-beads falling out of them.

I parked in the spot next to him and peeked into his car — the doors unlocked, the engine still warm. Then I opened the trunk, taking the first-aid kit out of the corner where he always kept it. I held it under my arm, and tried to follow his footsteps to the oval groundside hole we all knew about in the back fence (still there) and over to the hill. The place was now entirely deserted — silent. Even from a distance, I could make out his shadow's form. I knew where to look.

I walked quickly, deliberately, back to where we were sitting the other night. And there Josh was: right up close, lying on his back, by himself. His suit jacket and keys in a pile beside him. A large blue flashlight.

I stood there above him because I thought, at first, he wasn't going to say anything.

But he surprised me. "Do you think it's safe for you to be wandering around closed public spaces like this?" he asked.

I was still standing. "It's not unsafe," I said. "Which may be one of the few benefits of coming home again."

"Not a bad one, I guess," he said. He sat up, taking a closer look at me, noticing the first-aid kit in my hand. "What happened here?" he said.

"I need you to fix me," I said. Then I moved his pile of things out of the way and sat down where they'd been, taking my flip-flop off. He reached over and picked my damaged foot up, cradled the heel in his hand.

"What did you step in exactly?" he said.

"Exactly one broken Amstel Light bottle," I said. "I think it split open inside my foot. I'm sure there are still some slivers in there. Maybe now slivers of the slivers."

He shone the flashlight on it, pushing on the wound lightly with the tip of his finger.

"It doesn't look too bad," he said.

"It's not too great," I said.

But as I said it, I started thinking of Josh's first year of medical school. I had gone to stay with him, and was flipping through one of his books. What was that line I read that always stayed with me? *The body can accommodate all types of foreign objects as long as you need it to do so.* I started to ask now if that was true — if I were remembering correctly or revising it somehow. But I decided to just let it be true, for the next two minutes, especially because that wasn't even my real question. My real question was, How did the body do that? How did it learn what to hold on to, and when to let go?

Josh took out a pair of tweezers and some gauze, and started patting down the area. "In case you're wondering," he said, "I came back here because all I wanted in the world was to be somewhere very, very quiet."

I pulled my foot back as soon as the metal touched. "Is that your way of telling me that I'm out of here after you do this?"

"That's my way of saying no screaming."

I gave him back my foot. The flashlight was shining off his face, making him look both younger and older than usual: a stern face staring back at me, trying hard to concentrate.

"So is it the most awful time to ask you what you're planning to do now?" I said.

He stayed quiet for a while, staying focused on my foot, the tweezers before him.

"I know I'm a bad guy," he said.

"You're not a bad guy, Josh," I said. "A bad guy would have gone through with it."

"But a good one wouldn't have let things get that far in the first place." He shrugged, offering a half-smile. "I just keep thinking that I'm not the kind of guy you root for."

"Not yet maybe," I said, but I smiled back at him when I said it. Because he almost was. Or maybe because I believed that he could be. Inside, I was still really sure of that.

"It was weird earlier, you know? I always thought that when I actually got to the wedding day, I'd remember all the reasons I'd loved her, and that would be enough to carry me through."

"That didn't happen?"

"No, that was exactly what happened. But it was like the opposite effect. When I loved her the most, I realized it just wasn't enough."

I bent my knee, moving my foot closer to him, making it easier for him to get to the base of it. "I'm going to pull now," he said. "It will feel like a tight pinch, but that's it."

This was of no comfort to me. Josh had told me a long time ago that "pinch" was the word he told his patients when he really meant pain. I was going to tell him so, but it was nice watching him focus. Even when the "pinching" started. It made me remember something else about him. Something beyond all this.

"When are you heading back to Rhode Island?" I said.

He hesitated for a minute, but I could see it in his face. He knew exactly. "Tomorrow morning."

I nodded, and stayed quiet. I wanted to ask him about the rest of it. I wanted to ask if he thought she'd let him stay, if he thought he even deserved that chance to try to work things out. But that really didn't seem like the point. The point was that he knew where he wanted to go. For once, on that, he was clear. And he was actually doing something about it. Something brave. And that made me proud of him.

"Maybe you can come down to Narragansett in the next couple of weeks and help me move out." He looked up at me, and I could see the questions in his face: I was packing it in? Just like that? No more wives? No more any of it? "It's funny, isn't it?" I said. "Just when Mom and Dad are finally going to get me out of Rhode Island, you're going in."

"I'm sure they'll find it hilarious," he said. He shook his head, taking one last tug. It hurt so much, it almost burned. "God, can you picture Mom coming to visit me there? She'll have a heart attack when she sees those dogs."

I thought of how Josh had looked at the farm with Elizabeth and Grace: so certain, ready. I knew now that *that* was all she wanted for us — that kind of hope. "Yes," I said. "I can."

Josh put the tweezers away and wrapped my injury in two thick layers of gauze, tightly wound tape. Then he gave my foot a little pat to signify that my mini-surgery was complete.

"I'm all set?"

"You're all set."

I shook my foot out, which was looking a little like an oversize snow cone. It felt pretty good though.

"Are we not going to talk about it?" Josh asked, trying to catch my eye. "How you're leaving the wives project behind?"

My wives project. All of it resting in its new home on the side of the Hutchinson

River Parkway. I felt a pinch again, thinking about it. But, the truth was, even 900 wives wouldn't be able to do what I'd thought I needed: they couldn't make my first love story end happily. And they couldn't tell me how to move on, until I actually started moving. It was a nice thing, at the very least, that I didn't need them to anymore. And maybe an even nicer thing that they had taught me something after all — not about figuring out how to wait, of course. But about living, fully, even while you're waiting for whatever it is you think you want.

"Whenever you're ready to start with your I-told-you-so lecture, Josh," I said, "let me know. I'll just close my ears."

He shook his head slowly. "No, you know what? I think I'm going to pass."

I smiled, and watched as he gathered up his things, picked up the flashlight, and stood — stretching his arms out. Then, with his free hand, he reached down to pull me up to standing too. "I just don't know how you walked around with that in your foot all day," he said. "It seems like a fairly painful enterprise."

"Well, I think both of us have been creating some pain for ourselves for a while now," I said.

He rolled his eyes at me, which I guess I deserved. "Can we save the philosophizing, please?" he said.

"Sorry. It felt like the moment was calling for it."

He turned the flashlight on, shining it at my face for a second, before motioning with it in the direction of the parking lot. We started heading that way, Josh staying about half a step behind me. In four weeks though, on my way to Los Angeles, I would come back here to take a photograph. I'd want to remember how I had felt sitting here — to take it with me, this sense of relief I knew we were both feeling, the quietly growing momentum that eventually I'd understand comes from letting go of the things you were holding on too tightly to in the first place. But it was daytime when I came back, and everything felt different. In our spot was an enormous rainbow umbrella, the edges of two red beach towels sticking out from beneath it. It seemed important to take the picture anyway. So I did. From the angle I shot it, you could only make out the top of the umbrella: a swirl of bright colors against the August sun, intense and glowing, but distant from me, benign. Which, really, turned out to be the most hopeful epilogue to the weekend, to the whole crazy time, that I could hope for.

"So did you ever figure out my toast, by the way?" Josh said now, falling in step beside me. "What you were going to say today, if you ended up having to stand up and say something?"

"I didn't get that far." I shrugged. "But I probably would have kept it pretty short."

"How short?" he said, starting to smile. I could hear the amusement creeping up in his voice, the familiar sarcastic tone.

He was enjoying himself way too much. I smiled back anyway though, mostly because it didn't matter anymore — what I would have said, or would have done. Other things mattered more now. There are words and there are feelings and somewhere between where the two meet is the truth. Here was my truth: I was ready to go home. We were both ready for that, I thought, and — finally, *finally* — for whatever was coming next.

I stopped walking, but only for a second. "Just, you know, the really important things," I said. "Be well, be happy, be true. And, then, of course . . . cheers."

This was when I raised an imaginary glass in my hand, gave it all one last moment, and kept going.

The employees of Thorndike Press hope you have enjoyed this Large Print book. All our Thorndike and Wheeler Large Print titles are designed for easy reading, and all our books are made to last. Other Thorndike Press Large Print books are available at your library, through selected bookstores, or directly from us.

For information about titles, please call:

(800) 223-1244

or visit our Web site at:

www.gale.com/thorndike
www.gale.com/wheeler

To share your comments, please write:

Publisher
Thorndike Press
295 Kennedy Memorial Drive
Waterville, ME   04901